IF YOU'VE STEPPED IN S#1T, SPREAD OUT YOUR TOES

THUS SAID PRANCHÚ

DANIEL CASI

PUBLISHED BY
Amazon

FIRST EDITION
September 2021

ILLUSTRATION BY
Eduardo Garcês Viana

TRANSLATION BY
Carolina Nascimento Fernandes

LAYOUT AND GRAPHIC PROJECT BY
Érica Cristina Ferreira dos Santos

Dados Internacionais de Catalogação na Publicação (CIP)
(Câmara Brasileira do Livro, SP, Brasil)

```
Casi, Daniel
   If you've stepped in shit, spread out your toes
[livro eletrônico] : thus said Pranchú! / Daniel
Casi. -- Brasília, DF : Ed. do Autor, 2021.
   PDF

   ISBN 978-65-00-29157-5

   1. Aforismos e apotegmas 2. Filosofia 3. Poesia
4. Reflexões I. Título.

21-77764                                      CDD-800
```

Índices para catálogo sistemático:

1. Literatura   800

Cibele Maria Dias - Bibliotecária - CRB-8/9427

PHILOSOPHICAL ECHOS

ARNALDO NISKIER
Brazilian Academy of Letters

We lose our appetite for living when our passions are satisfied. The passion for reading, however, can never be satisfied, as it is not limited to the realm of words. This book by the writer Daniel Casi illustrates how talents can be reinvented and nurtured. With competence, authenticity and humor, the tales of Thus Spoke Pranchú are interdisciplinary in theme and good-natured in disposition.

By imagining a philosopher from the Northeast of Brazil who is "all knowing and ever present", inspired by Nietzsche's Thus Spoke Zarathustra, Casi provides appetizing plots and curiosities that spark his audience's desire to read.

In his adventures, the imaginary philosopher Pranchú makes his way through "Dante's Inferno", has "Dialogues with Aristotle", takes on Descartes' "Discourse on Method", in addition to comparing Exupéry's and Machiavelli's "Princes". In his anthropological or philosophical "analyses", Pranchú isn't pleased with only dialogue, he seeks deeper understanding. With humor and irony, his desire is to make permanent what is transitory.

The memoirist Pedro Nava said that experience "is a lighthouse facing backwards." It is thanks to my experience and life of teaching that I'm able to recognize talents and vocations from a distance. This book is a pleasant surprise, which I happily recommend.

Rio de Janeiro, November/ March 26th, 2019.

AUTHOR'S NOTE

An inspired drunkard, still in a state of incomplete drunkenness (euphoria), attributes his philosophical ramblings to an intellectual. Some might recognize the mentioned intellectual while others might not, despite being aware of and remembering the picturesque or folkloric phrase quoted by the drunkard. After all, many of these phrases are based on popular wisdom or on the collective unconscious. At that exact moment, a totally unexpected author would emerge. His name? Pranchú.

But who is this rascal called Pranchú?

It all started with a joke. When someone would say something really profound and philosophical, Pranchú would emerge to add in his moral axioms, though almost always immoral, which stemmed from a very biased, comical and wordy philosophy, as Pranchú himself would say. His wisdom, concealed within its simplicity and various catchphrases, served to heat up debates, to highlight certainties, to make friends, to influence people or to simply ease the hardships of everyday life.

Early on, Pranchú's phrases expressed the most bizzare of thoughts and also the wisdom of the Brazilian Northeast, a region different from many others in the country and in the world. Over time, some recognized Pranchú through his exotic quotes and asked who he was. The answer was always the same: Pranchú was an all-knowing and ever-present philosopher from Paraíba, Brazil who took part in practically all the historical episodes of our region and of the world. Without even knowing it, Pranchú had become a character who already had a life of his own.

Although responsible for his autonomy, Pranchú still needed to find his place in the sun, especially in this very disruptive world in which we live. Actually, why not be disruptive as well? It was with precisely this in mind that *Thus Spoke Pranchú* emerged, interrupting the normal course of a creative process and finding its way into a brand new one, which itself was a total disruption. Pranchú evolved and became an idea based on a question: how did the great thinkers of humanity get insight for their greatest works? The answer was obvious: with Pranchú's intervention at the perfect moment.

The all-knowing, ever-present and timeless philosopher Pranchú, the object of this book, thus began coexisting with great thinkers at crucial points in their lives.

Contact with Pranchú, however brief, was enough to help these thinkers develop their great works. Pranchú and his incredible ability to cause changes in pre-established models in our society and in people sowed the seed of what would one day be called *innovation*. When he was with humanity's greatest thinkers, Pranchú became disruption itself.

The idea behind creating Pranchú, therefore, was to imagine how a thinker, philosopher or artist came up with a striking idea. In other words, how did these gifted people end up leaving behind, as their legacy, such important ideas for the rest of humanity? Ideas are abstract, mental representations with adjacent concepts which can serve for something or for absolutely nothing. Still, the ideas of those great thinkers changed the course of humankind.

It is in those crucial instants that Pranchú appears to justify the thinker's moment of epiphany and disruption. It's as if his brief acquaintance with someone were enough to totally change that person's life, enough to make them reinvent themselves at some point. Pranchú provokes the fracture of pre-established patterns and processes, similar to what there is nowadays.

At some point or another, Pranchú coexisted with great thinkers, poets, and artists such as Agatha Christie, Aristotle, Basquiat, Beauvoir, Bukowski, Dostoevsky, Foucault, Gregório de Matos, the Brothers Grimm, Osho, Plato, Rousseau, Rui Barbosa and Sartre, and he has also alluded, in practical terms, to the thoughts of Dante Alighieri, Machiavelli, René Descartes, Hegel, Saint-Exupéry, among others. The aim of this book is to imagine how insight was sparked in the mind of great thinkers for their greatest works or how the work of these thinkers can be practical in everyday life.

Moreover, it is an invitation to the curiosity behind insight or to what a great thinker really wanted to express with their ideas. It is an even greater invitation to disruption, to imagining exactly what went on when thinkers challenged pre-established concepts and caused behavioral changes in the way people were previously thinking and acting. And Pranchú was there in every eureka moment.

It was also necessary that Pranchú wander around in order to meet all these thinkers, despite the fact that he was only human, too human in fact. That's when the most wandering wanderer appears, especially since he was considered the very first immoralist in history. It was Zarathustra, written about by Nietzsche. Truly, the first immoralist in history was Pranchú, as you will see in the book, but Zarathustra was the perfect reference point for our philosopher from Paraíba.

The book uses poetic and fictional form to explore some of Nietzsche's ideas, such as Zarathustra's main idea that humans are a transitional form between apes and what Nietzsche literally called "overman", usually translated as "superman". The name Zarathustra is one of many puns in the book and most clearly refers to the image of the sun rising over the horizon at dawn as the simple notion of victory.

The personification of Zarathustra is similar to the personification of Pranchú, only with a slightly different focus. The book *Thus Spoke Zarathustra* is told in episodes, with elaborate language, and always ends with a moral aphorism. Similarly, the idea behind Pranchú, a paraphrase of *Thus Spoke Zarathustra*, was to tell the wanderings and teachings of the all-knowing, ever-present philosopher, prophet, and *mugangeiro* from Paraíba in his most diverse incursions. Some stories are humorous, some are in a more serious tone, others are told in more elegant language, but at the end of each text there is always a moral aphorism or funny maxim.

The purpose of writing these texts was to present a positive, comical, and reflective response to the various setbacks that life imposes on us, all founded on the biased philosophies of Brazilian bumpkins and on the spirit from the Northeast of the country. For further philosophical nuance, the short stories evidently have quotes from recognized philosophers and each title, in general, adopts a slightly more formal tone, as it is precisely the contrast between formality and humor that sets apart what has become *Thus Spoke Pranchú*.

Surveys amongst peers and beers were carried out, mainly in establishments which provide recreational ethanol consumption and have their own on-call philosophers. Pranchú, all philosophy and poetry, has become a mysterious entity in the collective unconscious because of his moral teachings. Don't expect to make much sense of his aphorisms, as many of them truly transcend common sense. And even if they do mean nothing, they have an interesting effect, especially after a few good shots. Do, however, understand that there is a Pranchú in each one of us, after all:

> *"Ignorance and innocence are one and the same: they both believe in everything because they doubt nothing."*

Thus said Pranchú!

TABLE OF CONTENTES

"IT WOULD BE WORSE IF IT
WERE WORSE. IRONICALLY,
AS IF BY FATE, A TREE WEPT
WHEN IT SAW THAT THE
HANDLE ON THE AX WAS
MADE OF WOOD."

AS IT IS SAID...IT IS DONE!

There was a large crevice on the ground and, in it, one could find an immense pool of calm, unsuspecting waters. Below the crevice and near this pond, there was a natural shelter, no more than a small cave, with palpable warmth. The bushes surrounding it were prodigiously taken care of by nature itself and served as shade during sunset. A few fruit trees were at the back of the cave, as if produced in their own backyard. The access to this place was difficult because to get there, one needed to descend a considerable depth without communicating or making any noise that resembled civilization. Due to its remoteness, the place was home only to a few birds, some small reptiles and some fish. It was the perfect environment for a hermit, although none had appeared until that moment.

On that day, the scenery was akin to that of a spring painting lost in a distant past. The spot, until then unexplored, would now be inhabited by two illustrious strangers who had never met.

The first to arrive came from far away. His name was Zarathustra (Zoroaster), of the Spitama family from Iran, old Persia, the sixth son of Pourushaspa and Dugdav Spitama. He had been on a solitary journey for ten long years, had not eaten any food of animal origin, and wandered in isolated places for the sole purpose of reflecting on his visions and ideas. Zarathustra's reflections were far from simple and included questions such as: Who had made the sun and the stars in the sky? Who had created water and plants? And who had invented that the moon should wax and wane? Who implanted natural goodness and justice in people? Questions only a madman could think about in that isolated place.

The second to arrive, following the same trail of tranquility and total immersion within his own essence, was the intoxicating Pranchú. He was an all knowing and ever present philosopher from Paraíba[1] who represented the vivid imagery and philosophies of the *sertanejo*[2] man, a genuine expression of the Northeastern spirit in Brazil. During that same period, Pranchú was also looking for a place to reflect and philosophize far away from people, or as the Portuguese poet Alexandre Herculano would say: *"the more I know men, the more I value animals."* Pranchú sought to be alone just like a self-absorbed animal.

Zarathustra and Pranchú decided to isolate themselves at exactly the same period, in exactly the same setting. The only thing that separated them inside that crevice was the gigantic pond, as they were in distant, opposite corners. Each one had organized their shelter in front of what nature freely offered there. Despite not being able to see each other, they could hear sounds coming from the echoes within the crevice. Since they were hermits and spoke absolutely nothing, sounds of speech were rare.

Zarathustra, beholder of the stars, meditated all day and stopped only to eat some fruit. In his reflections in that place, Zarathustra meditated about the existence of a supreme being, who had created two other equally powerful beings and shared his own nature with them. Of these two beings, Ormuzd (whose Greek name is *Oromastes*) seemed faithful to his creator and was considered the source of all good, while Ariman (*Arimanes*) rebelled and became the author of all evil on Earth. Ormuzd created man and gave him all the resources to be happy, but Ariman countered that happiness by introducing evil into the world and creating poisonous reptiles, plants and beasts. As a result, evil and good were mingled in all parts of the world, and the followers of good and evil – adherents of either Ormuzd or Ariman – began an incessant war. But it would not last forever. For Zarathustra, the time would come when the adherents of Ormuzd would be victorious and Ariman and his followers would be condemned to the depths of darkness.

When meditating on all of this, Zarathustra began to contemplate fire and the rising sun as emblems of Ormuzd, as he is the source of all light and all purity. Reeling with ecstasy from this reflection, Zarathustra was suddenly terrified when he saw an immense snake surrounding his shelter and immediately exclaimed, to scare off this emblem of Ariman:

---

[1] From Paraíba, a state in the Northeast of Brazil
[2] Someone who comes from the drylands of Northeastern Brazil

"Go away you entity of evil!"

The huge crevice reverberated in a great echo:

Evil, evil, evil, evil…

On the opposite side of the great crevice, Pranchú had been unpretentiously collecting sticks for his night fire when he heard the voices coming from the crevice. In an equally involuntary act or reflex of fear, Pranchú answered aloud:

"Evil? Fuck off! Koff, koff, koff"…

The echoed response startled Zarathustra, who now stopped to reflect. Was it Ariman wanting to overwhelm Ormuzd? What did that term (koff) mean? The term did not mean anything derogatory or did not represent evil. However, since Zarathustra was a peculiar figure, not to mention eschatological, he created the idea that the crevice, in fact, was a cave full of sacred voices. Then, after a brief reflective pause, he asked the mighty crevice:

"Are you a being of light?" Light, light, light…

Pranchú, no less startled by the situation, could only imagine one hypothesis: someone was playing a joke on him. He didn't answer the question that came from the echo and instead, since he was quite a curious man, dropped what he was doing and walked around the cave to try and find the author of the echo. The place was gigantic so it took almost the entire day to reach the other side.

As he got closer, he noticed that someone was meditating and talking softly in the cave, as if they were grumbling. It was Zarathustra, still pondering whether there was a person on the other side of the crevice or whether the cave was actually reverberating sacred voices. Zarathustra complained:

"Why doesn't the sacred cave answer me?"

Pranchú then realized the intensity of Zarathustra's reverie and queries, and thus decided to assume the figure of a sacred mentor, doing so by echoing his voice in that cave. He thought it could be a way of immersing himself in an area of knowledge foreign to him. If the point of being here was, after all, to reflect and philosophize, why not put that into practice? This was enough motivation for Pranchú.

The next day, when he had returned to his own shelter, Pranchú got started on his plan to drive his newfound neighbor towards hallucination, I mean, towards philosophical stimulation. Zarathustra was meditating near the great crevice when he suddenly heard a noise like a great thunder that reverberated throughout the cave. It was Pranchú, of course, using a blow horn made from animal parts he had found on his way to that place. To add to the sound effect, Pranchú also lit some torches and they began to reflect on the water, which gave the appearance of a strange glow.

Frightened by what he saw and heard, Zarathustra asked:

"Tell me, are you a being of light?" *Light, light, light…*

Pranchú, who had prepared his entire repertoire of answers, had the idea of using an invention created in ancient Greece. It was a cone-shaped mouthpiece wrapped in tanned animal hide which amplified the sound of a speaker's voice. It was known by the Greeks as the megaphone. Slowly, while trying to impress his neighbor, Pranchú responded in a Westernized, Ibero Romance language:

"*¡Soy tu mano y tu mente!*"

Zarathustra, still very frightened, asked:

"*¿Vohu Manah, la Buena Mente?*"

When Pranchú heard the reply, he exclaimed in a low voice:

"Besides being crazy, this guy is also deaf! Sure, it can be Vohu…"

In a great reflective pause, however, as if looking for a lesson about that moment, Pranchú promptly understood that he could not continue teasing his neighbor like this. He realized that the guy was looking for something affirmative about the spirit, as a need to love himself. Who, in their right mind, would be seeking reflections on the gnosiology of the world isolated in a crevice such as this? Being his audacious self, Pranchú came to the conclusion that he needed to release his friend's wandering spirit from the paradox of the search for freedom trapped in a desolate place. After considering all of this, Pranchú said:

"My young Padawan[3], 'if you want, you can find all the answers you are looking for and even the answers to more interesting questions within yourself. The all-creating and sustaining god has chosen you to share the news of his divinity with the beings he creates. Now that you know this, you can announce this liberating message to everyone".[4]

Zarathustra immediately connected the part about the "all-creating and sustaining god" to Ormuzd, as if the divine figure were answering his wishes. But then, an imminent doubt struck him:

"Why me? I have no power or resources!"

There was a pause and then Pranchú answered:

"You have everything you need, which is what everyone else also has - good thoughts, good words and good deeds."

The words immediately struck Zarathustra and he began to reflect on morality, compassion, piety, loving neighbors and virtue. The time had come for great sacrifices! Pranchú's words rang out and Zarathustra fell silent, withdrew himself from that place, stepped outside the crevice and apparently intended on returning to civilization. Pranchú felt content with what he had done, and thought out loud:

"An ugly stone in need of a sculptor![5] I hope that he can be the sculptor himself and that he doesn't shy away from shaping himself."

Zarathustra went home and told everyone what had happened to him. His family welcomed the new discoveries, but the priests rejected them all. Accepting Zarathustra's thoughts would dismantle the whims of those priests, which led them to determine an end to Zarathustra's life. The philosopher, in turn, decided to run away and continue his simple way of living elsewhere.

---

[3] Philosophical term that would only gain its Jedi meaning thousands of years later

[4] Bulfinch, Thomas. O livro de ouro da mitologia: a história de Deuses e Heróis. 10ª Edição. Rio de Janeiro: Editora Ediouro, 2000.

[5] NIETZSCHE, Friedrich. Ecce Homo: Como alguém se torna o que é. Tradução, notas e posfácio de Paulo César de Souza. São Paulo: Companhia das Letras, 1995, p. 89/93.

Zarathustra thus began explaining all the events in the world, always through the *good mind* and the knowledge he had acquired. His honesty and simplicity enchanted people and they started listening to him with open hearts and minds. Zarathustra's revelations and prophecies became the precursors of Zoroastrianism, one of mankind's oldest religions.

Thousands of years later, a German philosopher named Friedrich Wilhelm Nietzsche decided to resurrect Zarathustra to the world. He did so by narrating Zarathustra's wanderings, teachings and interpretations of the *overman*, that is, a fictional superman who became victorious by means of values connected to moral interpretations of existence. Little did Nietzsche know that the metaphysical and Manichean values preached by Zarathustra had been instilled in him by Pranchú some time in the past.

Still, the question humanity asks itself is: why would Nietzsche have chosen such an unlikely protagonist (Zaratustra) to appear in the pages of one of his major works, which is considered so exotic and enigmatic? After all, who was Zarathustra to Nietzsche and why choose him to star in a work of philosophy that was intended to transform people's values? The answer to this question was actually explained by Nietzsche himself:

"Zarathustra was the first to see in the struggle between good and evil the essential wheel in the working of things. The translation of morality into the metaphysical, as force, cause, end in itself.[6]"

Evidently, Nietzsche did not intend to create any kind of mystical vindication for dogmatism or transcendence with his Zarathustra (Zoroaster). Quite the contrary! According to Nietzsche, Zarathustra was the inventor of morals precisely because he was the greatest challenger of a universal moral order, called the "first immoralist", or in other words, the greatest challenger of convenient, established truths.

Nietzsche set this ungodly protagonist in one of his major "moral annihilating" pieces of work precisely because he considered Zarathustra to have been the first, all-too-human, superman. Not only does Nietzsche's Zarathustra denounce the

---

[6] NIETZSCHE, Friedrich. Thus Spake Zarathustra. Translated by Thomas Common December, 1999. Public Domain. Available: http://www.dominiopublico.gov.br/download/texto/gu001998.pdf.

farce of Christian morality, the morality of compassion, which sickens and weakens affirmative will, he also points out new values, making himself a destroyer as well as a creator. To him, values are actually human and therefore constructed and overturned by man, who gives effect and meaning to such values. Human, truly very human - thank god!

It so happens that, contrary to what Nietzsche assumed, the first immoral man in history was not Zarathustra, but Pranchú. In his unique way, the philosopher from Paraíba propagated morality, compassion, pity, loving neighbors, and Christian virtue through Zarathustra, so revered by Nietzsche. Pranchú was immoral, though, because he had broken his own paradigms by being compassionate to the lost Zarathustra. In other words, Pranchú, a scoffer by nature and shameless by choice, decided instead to tell Zarathustra unfinished truths so the latter could begin his construction.

For this reason, Nietzsche's Zarathustra is a mirror of Pranchú and should not be seen as a prophet who proclaims truths that are ready to be taught. Like Pranchú, Zarathustra is the master of his own truth and his own eternal return, as one who learns by teaching the lessons of life, which is an act of educating oneself and, in the course of this process, finding oneself day by day. Here lies the great lesson of the two philosophers, because, in the crazy society we live in today, people try to live like the random leaders or masters they see before even trying to understand themselves. Just take a look at today's social networks.

Looking inside oneself demands a need for an encounter, for achievements, for experiences, for what is desired and what is wanted, as well as the wisdom to deal with indifferent, unfeasible and non-experiences, with the passing of time and with what is tenuous and provisional. It is about understanding the movement of life, its developments and its journey which reveal a great connection between Zarathustra and Pranchú, through a timeless and liberating dialogue with Nietzsche.

In the uniqueness of the encounter between Zarathustra and Pranchú, there was a difference reigning in both their lives, a difference that would become evident in the course of their lives after their encounter in that large crevice in the ground. Nietzsche explains that Zarathustra, at the age of thirty, had left his village and gone to the mountains. It was during this time he had met Pranchú. Ten years later, after having enjoyed his spirit and his solitude, Zarathustra finally grew tired of his own wisdom and, at sunrise, got up and said:

"Oh great star! What would be joyous to you if there was no one for you to enlighten? [...] Look! I have had enough of my own wisdom, like a bee that has gathered too much honey [...] I want to donate and distribute [...] So I must go down to the depths."

Thus said Zaratustra!

Nietzsche commented that Zarathustra had grown tired of his wisdom, which consisted in elevating his thoughts and reflections away from the world, and therefore decided to share his sapience with the world. Zarathustra became a master who proposed to teach through interpellations. Pranchú, however, was an accidental pedagogue, a kind of involuntary artisan, who inspired others more than he was inspired himself. He did everything in an unreasonable way. He was a gardener of dilemmas, an awakener of insights, an installer of "turning points"[7] and, above all, a fisherman of dreams. Zarathustra sought inspiration to be a master and Pranchú became a master without ever seeking inspiration.

If he could have heard Nietzsche's paraphrase of Zarathustra growing weary of his own wisdom, Pranchú would certainly consider the great irony of abdicating distant thoughts while sharing present ones, as if they were different from each other. Thus, amending Zarathustra in the quote above, Pranchú would say:

"It would be worse if it were worse. Ironically, as if by fate, a tree wept when it saw that the handle on the ax was made of wood."

Thus said Pranchú!

---

[7] Turning point is an expression used in psychology which means a decisive or critical moment, which indicates a moment in which something very important and decisive occurs in someone's life, whether it be for good or bad, and which becomes a mark that will change this person considerably

"IT IS BY DOING AND SPEAKING A LOT OF SHIT THAT WE FERTILIZE LIFE!"

◊2

THE SILVER SOPHIST

It was always in the Athenian lyceum that the great thinkers of classical philosophy emerged. Nevertheless, philosophical discussions also took place outside the academy after some friends and nerds by nature decided to create a study group they named *The Friends of Wisdom*.

The contemporaries Protagoras (Prota), Gorgias (Gorgi), Prodicus (Dicus), Hippias (Pi) and Pranchú (Pran) founded the group *The Minds of Wisdom*, which soon after was also known as *The Lies of Wisdom*, a term that originated in a philosophical school named *The Sophist School* (IV and V B.C.), in Ancient Greece. Those who belonged to the group were called sages, from the Greek word *sophiste*, and mastered the techniques of rhetoric and speech.

The objective of *The Minds of Wisdom* was to create a movement that would express something that all poorly diagrammed subjects had yet to experience. As they were nerds expanding their theoretical knowledge without any real life experience, the group intended to work hard in the art of rhetoric to create discourses about experiences they had not yet been through. It was a way of softening the fact that, despite having a lot of technical and philosophical knowledge, no one in their group had ever left Greece or had any experience of life outside of Greece. As they had no experience in anything, they would use sophism and their imaginations. For this reason, the group was not concerned with the search for the truth, but only with the art of winning arguments through rhetoric. The rest was nonsense!

To go further into their objective, the nerds created an awards system: best speaker, best use of rhetoric, syllogisms or deductive arguments in a speech, and - the most coveted award of all - *The Silver Sophist*. The award was so significant that they would perform any sort of rhetoric to get it.

The Silver Sophist award was based on their shared admiration for the father of dialectics, the philosopher Heraclitus of Ephesus, the most radical dialectical thinker in ancient Greece. For him, everything is in constant change and conflict is the father and king of all things. He also argued that life or death, sleep or wakefulness, youth or old age are realities that transform into each other. His 91st fragment, the most famous, stated that "a man does not bathe twice in the same river." This is because on the second time, he will not be the same man and neither will he be in the same river - for both will have changed.

Well, based on sophistry and dialectics, the so-called orators of nothingness, the nerds Prota, Gorgi, Dicus, Pi, and Pran, began the battle for the first *Silver Sophist* award.

Prota, one of the first speakers in Greece, liked to use rhetoric in a relativistic way, that is, to use rhetoric for absolutely nothing. For him, things were known in a particular and very personal way for each individual, which is why everything was fair and relative.

Gorgi was a natural speaker. In the future, he would travel through the cities of Greece just to demonstrate his oratory skills and get paid for them. He was responsible for innovations in rhetoric involving the structure and ornamentation of words and sentences, being the first to use paradoxical thinking in his rhetoric, that is, in the expression of contrasting ideas, in which the opposition, besides having inconsistencies, presented contradicting elements. He was a trickster of faith, which meant he believed in his own trickery.

Dicus was also an excellent speaker and would later become a professor. Unlike the other nerds, he focused on ethics. However, his ethics were necessarily negative and fragile, with rhetoric that highlighted the pains of life and hopeless resignation. He was the true preacher of tragedy!

Pi was an orator with infallible memory, perhaps because he had a background in mathematics, and this characteristic allowed him to be the best paid of all the orators later in the future. He was known for being vain and arrogant, as he considered himself to be a deep connoisseur of practically everything, from history and literature to craftwork and science. Evidently, mathematics was not suitable for a sophist, but it was just another detail he used to get ahead in the rhetorical battles. He was a braggart who liked to boast.

Pran, the most pragmatic orator, did not like to use words in vain, which gave him a disadvantage in the fight for *The Silver Sophist* award. He liked to question the usual beliefs of those with whom he conversed and subsequently, realizing his ignorance, would seek true wisdom. In his rhetoric, he always used irony and awareness of his interlocutor's ignorance, that is, he knew the importance of the ignorance of those with whom he conversed. He was a gardener of dilemmas! The biggest difference between Pran and the other nerds is that Pran had far greater travel experience than any of them ever knew.

The first rhetorical battle for *The Silver Sophist* had some rules. The speaker had to narrate a situation he had lived in other circumstances and end with a quote that expressed both that particular moment and some sophistic idea.

Prota, the rascal of relativity, was the one who started the fight. He narrated a long story set in lands beyond the sea, with adventures that bordered thresholds between the sacred and the profane. In his tale, he had walked, ran and swam many, many miles. Prota explained that the miles he had covered during the journey were different from the miles in Greece. A thousand miles across the sea is nothing, but a thousand miles in Greece would be almost everything. In the end, he synthesized his idea: "Man is the measure of all things: of the things that are, that they are, of the things that are not, that they are not."

Then Gorgi, the trickster of faith, began his explanation. He narrated a love story he had lived in Macedonia. Gorgi had met a beautiful maiden who was betrothed to another. They fell in love, but the maiden was forced to marry the other. Not wanting to perform any heroic deeds, Gorgi turned to his insignificance. Faced with the drama of life, the only consolation for Gorgi would be the word, which acquires its own value because it does not express the truth, but only the appearance of that moment. For Gorgi, words express in the best way the passions that guide the lives of men. And in the end, he concluded: "If it is eternal it has no beginning, if it has no beginning it is infinite, if it is infinite it is nowhere, if it is nowhere it does not exist."

Dicus, the preacher of tragedy, began his speech by narrating his wanderings in the lands of Corsica, in a commune called Aleria. In that region there was a great thinker who gave advice to anyone who asked. It was reported that a young man had asked him whether wealth was good or bad. His reply was that wealth was good for someone who was good and knew how to use it, and bad for worthless people who lacked knowledge. Dicus concluded his thoughts with the phrase: "The public recognition of an individual's worth is the measure of his usefulness."

Next, the vain Pi began his narrative about a journey through the Black Sea, in which he was an adventurer in both sea and land. His tale permeated the most diverse branches of scientific knowledge, starting with mathematics, moving towards geography, then history and ending up in biology. It was a professorial narrative in which the speaker was more concerned with boasting. In the end, he tried to justify that everything that happened emerged from beauty. His conclusion was that: "Beauty as convenience is no longer a specific object, but a kind of generator of the appearance of beauty. Beauty is nothing more than an appearance."

And finally it was Pran's turn. As the gardener of dilemmas, he first asked his counterparts a question before starting his presentation: how would they decide the winner of the award? Despite having created initial rules, the philosophers forgot to establish the criteria that would determine the winner. For them, rhetoric came before any dilemma. Prota, the oldest of the speakers, came up with a solution.

"Well, since Pran hasn't delivered his speech yet, why don't we choose him as the mediator and judge of this event? The criteria will be at his discretion. What do you all think?"

Everyone immediately agreed, including Pran himself, who was in no way willing to participate in that cauldron of deception. The nerds then decided that Pran should briefly comment on each speech and, with those considerations in mind, decide who would receive the award. Pran thus began his systematic analysis of each narrative.

"Prota, you well-known rascal from Abdera and its neighboring regions, you are very creative. I liked your maritime narrative, especially because a thousand miles would be worth nothing overseas, but in Greece it would be a lot. This echoes in your final phrase, which is truly striking - 'Man is the measure of all things.' It's beautiful. Too bad it doesn't say much, as if knowledge could be altered according to the changing circumstances of human perception. What's true for one person may not be true for another. A cockroach in front of others is harmless, but in your room it's a monster."

"Gorgi, you trickster from Leontini, you are also very good. I liked the maiden's tale, it's a pity that your heroism didn't go any further and only left enough room for sexual self-flagellation. Your final phrase was also remarkable - 'If it is eternal it has no beginning, if it has no beginning it is infinite, if it is infinite it is nowhere, if it is nowhere it does not exist.' But it does not say much either. You manage to destroy any possibility of reaching some truth. Our reason can only enlighten the situations men live in, it does not have the capacity to form absolute rules. The same activity can be good or bad depending on who does it and what the situation is. No wonder you abandoned that maiden. I would call that the stigma of a wimpy philosopher."

"Dicus, you tragic guy from the beautiful island of Ceos, you are as good as Gorgi and Prota. I liked the story of the great thinker from Aleria, especially when he was asked if wealth is good or bad. Too bad your conclusion doesn't say much either, especially when it comes to your final phrase - 'Public recognition of an individual's worth is the measure of his usefulness.' Your claim applies to practically everything in life. It seems you're saying that the nature of things depends on the nature of the doers. In other words, everything around a hole is a border or, depending on the situation, everything around the hole is a butt."

"Pi, you verbose, vain man from Elis. You're also very creative. I liked your adventurous journey across the Black Sea, especially the interdisciplinary nature of your story. In fact, your final phrase illustrated what you consider beauty - 'Beauty as convenience is no longer a specific object, but a kind of generator of the appearance of beauty. Beauty is nothing more than an appearance.' Too bad it also doesn't say much. Now, why would a beautiful thing need, in addition to being beautiful, a beautiful appearance? For you, beauty is nothing more than an appearance that imposes itself on everything. It was just an excuse for you to boast, that's all! It's like that old saying, 'the one who determines the quality and the name of a wine is its label.'"

Everyone was shocked by Pran's comments, for it was as if their efforts had been worthless. Prota then asked:

"Pran, every argument allows for the discussion of two contrary theses, including this one in which favorable and contrary theses are equally defensible. With that in mind, who do you think won the award?"

"Gentlemen, honestly, I don't know who is the best. There was too much dialectics and not enough psychotropics! You're not simply swindlers, as this figure cannot be reduced to the phenomena you each narrated. You are keepers of a peculiar art: you have shrewd instinct, quick thinking and constant eloquence. In short, I would say that you are keepers of the so-called 'art of deception.' You are magicians of a reality everyone wants to hear. There is no winner in this art."

Gorgi, taking the floor, sophistically stated:

"Well, the being does not exist, if it did, it could not be recognized. Even if it were recognized, it could not be communicated to anyone. In other words, there is no way to define the winner given the fact that we didn't decide on the criteria for the award. What do you think?"

Dico, supporting Gorgi's proposal, made a ratification:

"I think Gorgi's proposal is valid, but I believe that Pran should give the final verdict on this issue, after all he did not participate in the event."

Everyone agreed and Pran now had to think of a conclusion.

"Very well, what is the use of clarity if objectivity is foolishness? For *The Minds of Wisdom*, lies and truths are not separated by centimeters, as the distance of these points requires measurements of another order. For you, portions, proportions and disproportions are subjects potentialized through caricatures of rationality. The fact, however, is that for some, deception is the ingredient and the spice for life. After all,

"It is by doing and speaking a lot of shit that we fertilize life!"

Thus said Pranchú!

"THE ONLY WAY TO CURE
PLATONIC LOVE IS TO FUCK
HOMERICALLY!"

◊3

FROM SMOKING TO FUCKING: AN ESSAY ABOUT PLATO'S CAVE[8]

"My noble Pranch, what is this wild place? If I didn't know you any better, I'd surely think you're mad!"

"Well, Plato, wasn't it you who told me you wanted to go to an appropriate place to reflect on metaphysics, gnoseology, dialectics, and mysticism? This is an excellent place to do just that."

"But did it have to be this dark and fetid cave? Couldn't it have been a mountainside, a cove, a boat, or really another place with a little more air? Frankly, this place is totally disconnected from the world and has nothing to do with what I think. I've wasted my time! I could have been tossing around the old pigskin with Socrates or even having a cold drink with Dionysia[9]!"

"Don't get angry, Plato, relax. Wasn't it you who said that 'all that deceives, enchants'? Very well, this place deceives and therefore enchants. I myself have already made various observations around here with my friend Zoroastro, and we had the chance to discuss beliefs such as paradise, resurrection, the final judgement, and the life of a messiah - you know, innocuous talks."

"Innocuous talks? You think that discussing the final judgement is innocuous?"

"Everything depends on how the story is told, dear Plato. *We're here to seek the essential truth of things[10].*"

---

[8] Original title: *Essay on Pranchú, according to Plato.*
[9] Ale comes from Dionysius, Greek god equivalent to the Roman god Bacchus, the one from the vital cycles, the festivals, the wine, the insanity, and, above all, the intoxication which connects drunkenness with divinity.
[10] The search for the essential truth of things is one of the main objectives of Plato's philosophy

"And how do you think I'm going to seek the essential truth of things in this darkness, with no inspiration whatsoever?"

"Not to worry! I've already thought of everything. To arrive at this truth, I've brought us a nice snack - not exactly a banquet, though - which will help keep us strong. I've also brought this other little thing here!"

"What other little thing, Pranch?"

"Well, since the Law of the Twelve Tables (Lex Duodecim Tabularum or Duodecim Tabulae in Latin) has yet to regulate the matter as a transgression, I have here one of Satan's cigarettes to vaporize the environment and help inspire us. See, now we can get our inspiration and also avoid the terrible hunger this cigarette causes!"

"Only you, Pranch, to piss me off like this!"

Instinctively, Pranchú reached into his satchel and retrieved a tuft of cannabis[11] and a thin, silky skin. He rolled everything up with a single hand and the air of a Jedi master and made a giant cannabis cigar. With his other hand, Pranchú lit the grass using the old fire starter[12] technique. The notorious blunt was now lit and in full use!

After thirty minutes of a gravelike silence, the dialogue restarted with a more pleasant air!

"Hey, Pranch, I think you were absolutely right! This scenery is perfect for deep reflections. I can even discuss the final judgement and other easy topics. The environment has calmed me down enough to consider, at last, that *'when the mind is thinking, it is talking to itself.'* Look at those beautiful birds and their harmonious flock!"

"Oh, Plato, I don't think you're seeing it correctly, because that is not a flock of birds, but of bats! Nothing beautiful there."

---

[11] *Cannabis sativa*
[12] Lighting a fire by friction involving a stone and a harsh surface (another stone, the ground, wood)

"Who cares? It's the concept that matters!"

"What concept? Bats are bats, period! And all this darkness doesn't really contribute to that blurred vision of yours."

"Pranch, *we could easily forgive a child who is afraid of the dark. The real tragedy in life is when men are afraid of the light.*"

"Well, now everything is fucked. You're not making any sense."

"Imagine these beautiful birds…"

"Birds, my ass - they're bats, Plato!"

"Whatever! Imagine these bats, which live in a dark cave, discovering the world of lights out there. It would be like freedom from an internal prison and discovering the real essence of things beyond the sensitive world. It would be as if they had believed, ever since birth, that the world was a certain way and then found out everything was false, partial, and that there were other, completely different concepts."

"Man, I have no idea what you're talking about, but maybe there's some sense in it…"

"It's as if the bats were freed from their own ignorance! The bats that sing here don't sing like the ones out there!"

"Well holy shit, now the son of a bitch has lost it! Plato, drink a little water because you've reached the emotionally perturbed stage."

"Pranch, the bats free themselves from ignorance. *The soul wishes to fly back home to the world of ideas. It wants to free itself from the prison of the body.*"

"Oh god!"

"*There is nothing good nor bad other than these two things: wisdom, which is good, and ignorance, which is bad.*"

"There we have it - the man is now making the thing into poetry!"

"All men are poets when they're in love!"

"What's that, Plato?"

"There are no exceptions - everyone becomes a poet when love takes over them, even those with no culture."

"Ok, Plato, this conversation is taking a strange turn. We're here in the middle of a dark cave and suddenly you're talking about love, about being in love, and all that. We're friends, it's best we stop here!"

"That which we don't know is much more than all we do know."

"To hell with that! The only thing I know is that this weed is unveiling your unknown side! Stop talking shit and try to get back to yourself."

"Try to move the world. The first step is to move yourself."

"Fuck you! Now take your first step, move yourself and let's go home. You've passed the limits, you shameless stoner!"

Two weeks after this disconnected dialogue, Pranchú and Plato met in front of the Athenian School where the class of that time studied. A bit ashamed, Plato began:

"Dear, Pranch, I apologize for that day! I got too torpid and can't remember much. The only thing I remember is that I got home and wrote down some things about caves, discoveries, light, darkness, I don't know, things of that sort. The next day, when I decided to read my notes, I didn't understand anything. The notebook is there, under my desk, with a terrible stench of weed."

"It's alright, I think the smoke has reached your already maddened mind too quickly. But tell me something - what about all that talk of love and of being in love? I have no objections, but are you coming out *qualira*[13]?"

---

[13] *Qualira* = a word used in the Brazilian state of Ceará meaning homosexual

"Not at all, dear Pranch! Actually, I'm head over heels for a beautiful lady who lives by my house, her grace *Diotima of Mantinea*[14]. She is so special - all I want to do is worship her and can't think of touching her in any way, you know?"

"Did you at least speak to her?"

"No, dear Pranch, because the only desire I have is to worship her in a spiritual way, her life teaches me the genealogy of love. Perhaps that's the reason why I was saying such disconnected things in that cave. The reason is simple - I am suffering because of this love! A love in which touching is not the intention."

"Well, Plato, whether you're smoking weed or jerking off, you're a good fellow. In any case, there's a cure for your problem."

From this narrative, the philosopher and mathematician Plato drew deep wisdom about Pranchú's philosophy, which sparked the beginning of his philosophical ideas and two main works: *The Allegory of the Cave*[15] and *Platonic Love*[16]. From weed in a cave to the world of philosophy, Plato gave in to the teachings of Pranchú despite being taken over by an impossible love at the moment in his life, a love against his own nature. At that instant, Pranchú revealed the cure to Plato's problem of unrequited love:

"The only way to cure platonic love is to fuck homerically!"

Thus said Pranchú!

---

[14] *Diotima of Mantinea* was a philosopher and greek priestess with an important role in Plato's Banquet. The philosophy of Diotima is in the origins of the concept of platonic love. The only source which speaks of her is Plato himself and thus it is not possible to ascertain if she is a character in his book or a person who in fact existed. Nevertheless, nearly all of the characters in the platonic dialogues correspond to real people who lived in ancient Athens.

[15] The Allegory of the Cave was a very successful myth interpreted by Plato, symbolizing metaphysics, gnoseology, dialects, ethics, and platonic mysticism. On the whole, it is the myth that expresses Plato in an in-depth way, leaving behind many parallels with the current times. Source: REALE, Giovanni & ANTISERI, Dario. *História da Filosofia: Antiguidade e Idade Média*. Vol. I, São Paulo: Edições Paulinas, 1990, pág. 168.

[16] Platonic love, in its vulgar meaning, is every affectionate or idealized relationship in which the sexual element is abstracted, like in the case of pure friendship between two people. This definition, however, differs from the same concept of ideal love by Plato, Greek philosopher from Ancient times, who understood Love as something essentially pure and with no passions. Passions, according to Plato, are essentially blind, materialistic, ephemeral, and false. Love, within the platonic ideal, does not base itself in any interests (not even sexual), but only in virtue.

"IF YOU CAN SEE FROM FAR AWAY,
MY FRIEND, YOU MUST BE SOME
TYPE OF GYNECOLOGIST BECAUSE
IT WOULD MEAN YOU LOOK WHERE
THE SUN DOESN'T SHINE!"

RHETORIC OF PASSIONS[17]: A DIALOGUE BETWEEN ARISTOTLE AND PRANCHÚ

"*Madhouse!* It's the combination of the terms mad and house, which perfectly describes where your father, crazy old Nicomachus, comes from!"

This phrase was taken from the beginning of a prodigious conversation held in Athens, around the year 310 BC, when two students were discussing the attitudes of the younger student's father. They began by questioning the father's demands that his son commit to classes such as biology, zoology, math, physics, logic, metaphysics and many other subjects no different from the ones today.

"Professor Ribamar[18], from biology class, shouldn't have shown my grade to my father directly! If he'd given it to me sooner, maybe I could've used the skill I've actually learned, rhetoric, to my advantage. Maybe I could've changed my grade using the good old rhetoric[19] of doubt! After all, *'doubt is the beginning of wisdom'.*"

"Nice words, Ari! If you could really change your grade using rhetoric, I'd be your disciple forever. The problem is that a zero comes from very persuasive and universal language which is practically immune to rhetoric. Honestly, old friend, I think biology is just not your cup of tea."

---

[17] *Rhetoric of Passions* is the second work about Rethoric by the Greek philosopher Aristotle. What Aristotle is explicitly willing to show in his *Rhetoric* is that passion constitutes a key which a good orator will play in to convince. A horrible crime must arouse indignation, while a minor offense, absolutely forgivable, must be judged with compassion. To arouse such feelings, one must know the one that exists above all. There lies true passionate dialectic, which is always entangled in rhetoric with adjustments of differences, of contestations, which must find, in order to be persuasive, an identity, a political ideal of all interactions with others.

[18] Allusion to the great master Ribamar, exceptional biology teacher in the great Campina Grande region in Paraíba, Brazil.

[19] Rhetoric (from the Latin word *rhetorica*) is the art of using language to communicate efficiently and persuasively

"Yeah, but what can I do now? My father, that old brute Nicomachus, is going to eat me alive because of the grade and because of the lie I told him when I didn't have the courage to tell the truth. I can already see my punishment: he's going to take me to old Alexander's library and lock me in there for at least six months."

"Well, try to relax and look on the bright side. Maybe now you can take a moment to reflect on what you did! Lying, for example, is something that hurts morality and that is a part of ethics. I don't know, maybe you can think a little about *Nicomachean Ethics*[20]. And, since you'll be grounded in Alexander's library, you can think about how much nonsense you've been up to with all this *Rhetoric*[21] - one day it'll end up really phucking you up."

"I do like your suggestions. I'll be so isolated and alone, though. *'Whosoever is in solitude is either a wild beast or a god.'*"

"You won't be lonely, Ari! When no one ora pro nobis, maybe you can reflect On Virtues and Vices[22] and start the monologue of an onanist. It's an excellent reflection to have during sexual self-flagellation. And, if you're still not inspired, just remember the incentives we received that time we studied abroad in Rome from professor *Valeria Messalina Augusta*[23]".

"Oh Pran, my noble friend, I might actually propose this punishment to my father after all. You're absolutely right. *'The things we have to learn before we can do them, we learn by doing them!'* I know I'm going to get screwed in that shitty library, but it will be for a good cause and, after all, 'the roots of education are bitter, but the fruit is sweet.' I'm going to face that old brute of a father, Nicomachus, but I can already tell nothing good will come from it!"

---

[20] *Nicomachean Ethics* is considered Aristotle's main work about Ethics. It exposes the author's teleological and eudaimonist conception of practical rationality, his conception of virtue as median and his considerations about the role of habits and prudence.

[21] *Rhetoric* was written by the Greek philosopher Aristotle. It contains three books (I: 1354a - 1377b, II: 1377b - 1403a, III: 1403a - 1420a).

[22] *On Virtues and Vices (De Virtutibus et Vitiis Libellus*, in Latin) is the shortest of the four treaties on ethics attributed to Aristotle. The text, considered nowadays considered forged by academics and with uncertain origins, was probably created by a member of the Peripatetic school.

[23] Messalina was the wife of the Roman emperor Claudius. She was notorious for her adultery and for being unscrupulous. One time, she challenged Rome's main prostitute to a duel of who could have sex with the most men in a time frame of 24 hours. While the prostitute gave up in the middle of the challenge and said she couldn't go any further, Messalina continued for an additional 24 hours. She transformed the palace into a brothel and even tried to kill Claudius. Today, Messalina is the symbol of an easy, adulterous woman with no character. Source: http://www.dicionarioinformal.com.br/messalina/

"Madhouse!" It's the combination of the terms mad and house, which perfectly describes where your father, crazy old Nicomachus, comes from (initial dialogue)! I think that's why you're a little crazy and have your wits confused. All you need now, to complete this madness of yours, is to end up as a philosopher and an expert in biology[24], which is the subject you've failed. Wouldn't that be such an irony of fate!"

"Is that a provocation, Pran? We're good friends and I know that *'the wise man does not say everything he thinks, but always thinks everything he says.'*"

"Who am I to provoke anything, dear Ari! I'm just making a brief comment about some possibilities for our lives. Anyway, it's not prudent to provoke a madman like yourself. As a matter of fact, I have absolutely no doubt that, in order to cure your madness, you'll also find your way into the field of psychology[25]."

"That's a good idea too, Pran, as *'no great mind has ever existed without a touch of madness.'*"

"Indeed, Ari, but you're the kind of madman that not even Dr. Gardenal, the owner of that asylum in Athens, can save! In any case, if I were you, I would gather these aspirations and call Professor Plato, that old stoner who is always rambling nonsense, and invite him to go with you. Maybe you'll even create something together[26]!"

"Oh Pran, I really appreciate your suggestions, but you better stop giving me so many ideas! My mind is now bubbling with insights and I feel the need to drink

---

[24] In the year 343 AD, back in Athens, Aristotle founded the Lykeion, origin of the word Lyceum whose students became known as Peripatetic (those who walk), a name resulting from Aristotle's own habit of teaching outdoors, often under the trees that surrounded the Lyceum. Unlike Plato's Academy, the Lyceum favored the study of natural sciences. Alexander even sent the master copies of the fauna and flora of the regions he conquered. The work focused on the fields of classical knowledge of that time, philosophy, metaphysics, logic, ethics, politics, rhetoric, poetry, biology, zoology, medicine, and laid the foundations of such disciplines in terms of scientific methodology.
[25] Aristotle's works on psychology: On the soul; On Sense and Sensibilia (= Parva Naturalia 1); On Memory (= Parva Naturalia 2); On Sleep (= Parva Naturalia 3); On Dreams (= Parva Naturalia 4); On Divination in Sleep (= Parva Naturalia 5); On Length and Shortness of Life (Parva Naturalia 6); On Youth (= Parva Naturalia 7); On Breadth (=Parva Naturalia 8).
[26] Alongside Plato and Socrates, Aristotle is seen as one of the founders of Western philosophy.

a *Brejeira from Rhodes*[27] before lunch, and that is *'too good to think about'*[28]. You're such a great friend who helps me grow. I only have one more thing to tell you - despite my being short, know that 'if I can see from far away it's because I stand on the shoulders of giants.' Thank you for everything, my friend!"

And thus, history would have it that short little Ari would become the giant Aristotle, all because he was challenged by the ever present philosopher Pranchú and his subliminal teachings. At the end of their conversation, the prodigious Pranchú retorted the Aristotelian conclusion with a phrase that would one day become a Pranchurian moral:

"If you can see from far away, my friend, you must be some type of gynecologist because it would mean you look where the sun doesn't shine!"

Thus said Pranchú!

---

[27] Brejeira = liquor fabricated in the bogs, typically the bog in Paraíba, Brazil. cachaça fabricada no brejo, típica do brejo paraibano. Rhodes: the largest of the Dodecanese islands, located in the Aegean Sea and forming part of the territory administered by Greece; famous for the Colossus of Rhodes.
[28] Phrase used in the future by a philosopher from Pernambuco, Brazil named Chico Science.

"FUCKED, FETID, PENNILESS, AND
CAUGHT UP IN NONSENSE!
BUT DON'T BE SAD – THERE'S STILL
GOOD CARNIVAL OUT THERE!"

◊5

THE TOPOGRAPHY OF DANTE'S INFERNO

In matters of divine justice, there are three aspects to be avoided: malice, incontinence, and bestiality. The incontinent soul is guilty, the greatest guilt being that which comes from fraud, the will to sin. Malice degenerates the soul and bestiality makes one uncouth, or, as those in Goiás say, "Rough, rustic, and systematic!"

The colloquy above was the motif that originated the invitation. Pranchú's childhood friend, Dante, invited him to a brief incursion into the portals of hell, complete with *"Nine Circles, Three Valleys, Ten Moats, and Four Spheres"*, as very well illustrated by his namesake, Alighieri, in *The Divine Comedy*.

Very well, Dante was a friend of Pranchú's who lived in the historical city of Olinda, in the northeastern state of Pernambuco in Brazil. Since Carnaval was approaching, Dante invited his friend to spend the holiday at his house. He knew that Pranchú was not very interested in these kinds of festivities and because of this, challenged our philosopher. Pranchú would have to go to Olinda's Carnival party and afterwards describe in great detail this sabbatical ritual which he considered a true *inferno*.

To do so, Pranchú immersed himself completely in the Olindian carnival and elaborated a detailed description of Alighieri's *Inferno*, parodying the first part of The Divine Comedy in third person narrative. He entitled the Shrovetide *The topography of Dante's Inferno, according to Pranchú!*

Upon his arrival in the city, Pranchú noticed an alteration in people's state of mind, some with inebriant tendencies and others with changes in personality caused by contumacious drunkenness. Their altered state of mind made them lose their sense of decency and transmute into various well-known personalities. According to Pranchú, these were the "virtuous pagans[29]".

Pranchú noticed, as he walked along the city streets, that people wore costumes of pirates, clowns, pierrots, gypsies, and even Supreme Court justices in that region. Most people also had in their hand a yellow liquid, bubbly and perfectly chilled, as if it were a vital part of that ritual.

Within the crowd, there were musicians and people playing instruments who created an orchestra of insane harmonies without any connections. It was the devil's philharmonic, led by a so-called *Spok Orchestra*, which played apocalyptic trumpets to a bunch of mad people as they threw colorful paper strings at each other and carried giant mannequins in someone's honor.

From atop a great mausoleum, next to what seemed to be the epicenter of all the bedlam, a long-haired, bearded man appeared seated on a throne in the shape of a toilet. The man, who was not Jesus Christ - even though the presence of Our Lord was effectively needed in that instant - sang lively tunes that stirred the folks as in a real "cemetery of fire[30]."

> *"I have arrived at the four corners*
> *And everyone has arrived*
> *Going down the hill*
> *Lifting up the dust*
> *Stirring up the heat..."*

The deafening sound seemed to put people under spell and they couldn't stop chanting "hold me so I don't fall, hold me so I don't fall". Actually, many had already fallen because of the intoxication and were lying in the gutter, which alludes to a moral precept of "a dog which licks the mouth of a drunk", an idiomatic expression from one of Aesop's fables. While Pranchú pondered Aesop and his tender tales, he was taken aback by another nearly liturgical tune:

---

[29] The first circle of hell described by Dante Alighieri was the *Limbo*, also known as *virtuous pagans*. There, souls were fated to wander with no destination in complete darkness, where one cannot see anything, according to Dante, which represented minds that were never illuminated by the word of the Gospel. In Pranchú's context, *Limbo* is total drunkenness.

[30] Cemetery of fire, also known as *heresy*, was one of the circles of hell described by Alighieri. It was a cemetery for various heretic groups, among them the hairy Christ lookalike who sang hellish hymns. It was the grand master Alceu Valença adding fuel to the drunkenness.

"I fondly remember that ball
Where we danced so close to each other
Where we went only to hold each other"

It was the fable of *The Fox and the Grapes*, also by Aesop, sung by a badly diagrammed fellow with a head of curls and mischievous sunglasses. The fellow stood next to the aforementioned long-haired man, was well-humored and called himself the "King of the Land of Tackiness and yonder[31]".

Committed to furthering his knowledge on this sabbatical ritual, Pranchú asked his followers to join the strict traditions and customs of that set of rites, which included taking in that inebriating liquid and exchanging fluids with local maidens, as was determined by the authorities of that occasion.

In the village, the hills and alleys were taken by professional carnival groups which confronted each other seasonally with a single goal: achieving perfect originality. Because of this, the organizations had terribly curious nicknames: *Meanwhile in the Courtroom, I Don't Think That's Enough, Midnight Man, Black Lament, Mangrove Beat*, among many others. Pranchú could not understand why there was so much madness, but soon realized that the insanity was an ode in and for itself, like a hill of rocks[32]. The madness was such that Pranchú, beaten by his own philosophy, allowed himself to be intoxicated by the lunacy.

On the next day of the ritual, while resting in Dante the Joyful's humble hut, Pranchú was surprised by a mysterious set of activities orchestrated in the early morning. They were entitled "The Ruse", a curious play on words meant to rouse those who were still under the effects of insobriety. After a long, first day of clashing bodies and glasses, waking up with a hangover was not what Pranchú's had in mind for his research. Imagine his anger[33]!

Nevertheless, this version of Dante's hell did not only have ghouls and lost souls. There were also charitable souls, whose helpfulness was highly welcomed

---

[31] It was the eternal King Reginaldo Rossi.

[32] The hill of rocks, also known as greed, was found in one of the circles of Dante's Inferno. In this circle full of mountains, material riches became heavy weights in the form of golden bars and coins. One group had to push the weights against another group while exchanging insults, because they had opposing attitudes towards richness. To Pranchú, however, the greed in the street parties of Olinda's Carnival was linked to the group that wanted to show off more, as in "the worse, the better".

[33] Wrath, also known as the River Styx, was the fifth circle of Dante's Inferno.

in our philosopher's inquiries. Some of the maidens in that region, enchanted by Pranchú's physical and moral exorbitance, surrendered themselves to his sexual maintenance in an act of generous compassion towards the poor youth. There was so much charity and so many beautiful women in that valley of the winds[34] that Pranchú decided to tattoo the words "What a hound-filled hell!"

Fatigued by all the torment, hungover, and semen-less, Pranchú began to lose his exuberance and transition into a normal being - which sparked a new transformation. He could no longer follow the carnival rituals or even philosophize. He was in visceral need of a "cock's head[35]", a home remedy for all endemics, especially hangovers, limpness, and other carnival related convalescences. After stuffing himself with this delicacy, as if he were in a "lake of mud[36]", Pranchú at last resurrected and returned to his philosophizing.

In his descriptions, Pranchú stated that he witnessed attempts to steal (violence[37]) cans of fermented drinks, adulteration (fraud[38]) of beverages served to friends, and conjugal infidelity (betrayal[39]). These last references, however, did not influence Pranchú's evaluation of his first pilgrimage to the tormentous and dreamlike Carnival of Olinda.

In spite of being aloof to the event, Pranchú discovered that Carnival wasn't in fact invented by the devil, as some religions would have it. Perhaps it was invented by some religions, as some Olindian party-goers said! It is actually a festival of illusions, filled with a turmoil of emotions and good confusions. That's Carnival - all the grandeur of a splendid, glittery, and enthusiastic presentation. Then on Ash Wednesday, all citizens return to hell and see all their glee burn in an immense cauldron called routine.

---

[34] The Valley of the Winds, or lust according to Alighieri, was the judgment room where Minos, the judge of hell, heard the confessions of the dead - who always told the truth since they no longer had the gift of wit - and condemned them to a circle of hell. To do so, he would wrap his tail around himself according to the number of the circle to where the sinner would be sent off. Could you imagine what would happen if the sinner were condemned to pay with his own lust in Olinda's Carnaval? What a hound-filled hell that would be!

[35] This was a regional delicacy from the northeast of Brazil, especially in the states of Paraíba and Pernambuco, and was made with pirão (a thick broth made of cassava flour), eggs, cassava flour, and seasonings such as - and especially - pepper, onion, and cilantro.

[36] The Lake of Mud was the circle of gluttony. According to Dante, gluttons were immersed in their own vomit. If it were in Olinda, the ones immersed in vomit would be the drunkards.

[37] Violence, known as the Valley of the Fire, was the seventh circle of hell, according to Dante.

[38] Fraud, known as the Malebolge, was the eighth circle of hell, according to Dante.

[39] Betrayal, or Lake Cocytus, was the ninth circle of hell, according to Dante.

After finishing his research *in loco* and *in louco*, Pranchú declared what someday could be considered a moral precept of high relevance, especially to those who seek warmth, joy, contentment, ecstasy, and other synesthesia only the Carnival of Olinda could possibly conceive:

> *"Fucked, fetid, penniless, and caught up in nonsense!*
> *But don't be sad - there's still good Carnival out there!"*

Thus said Pranchú!

"CLEVERNESS WITHOUT JUDGMENT IS LIKE SAYING THAT BEAUTY IS A MATTER OF FAITH: THE INDIVIDUAL MAY EVEN BELIEVE HE IS BEAUTIFUL, BUT IT WILL BE QUITE DIFFICULT TO CONVINCE OTHERS!"

◇6

FROM THE LITTLE PRINCE TO THE PRINCE, FROM EXUPÉRY TO MACHIAVELLI: AN ANTHROPOLOGY OF *FULERAGEM*[40] IN BRAZIL ACCORDING TO PRANCHURIAN THEORY

Each society passes down the most obvious and basic anthropology of their cultural heritage. With Brazilians, it is no different. Ever since the year 1500, the History of Brazil has been marked by a policy that seeks to satisfy the most diverse of interests and a culture of favoritism which has continuously endorsed corruption and the like. Mercantilist practices and the predominance of economic interests over religious and ideological aspects has even reflected in what would become the definitive name of our land, as the writer of chronicles João de Barros protests: "by diabolical arts, the name of Santa Cruz, so pious and devout, was changed to that of a cloth dyeing stick (Brazil)[41]".

In the History of Brazil, the states and the mercantile bourgeoisies developed colonialist competition and set our coast as the stage for disputes between the Portuguese, the French and the Dutch. Throughout the rest of our history - from the goldrush, the era of coffee, the abolition of slavery, the establishment of the Republic and the New State, then later the Authoritarian Regime and finally down to the contemporary Age of Democracy - in all these moments, the culture of favoritism and corruption can be found, for it was rooted in those early Brazilian Colonies.

Now, one thing is the historical basis for this culture and another thing is the fact that it remains alive and well to this day. Nothing can justify the continuing improbity, corruption, and other chapters of the Penal Code which have been exposed in the recent culture of Brazilian history. Yet, knowing that nothing justifies any of this, how does a normal citizen today become corrupt? Apparently,

---

[40] Fuleragem is a Brazilian term from the Northeast of the country which means a lack of seriousness and refinery in behavior.

[41] BARROS, João de. Apud ALENCAR, Francisco; RAMALHO, Lúcia Carpi & RIBEIRO, Marcus Venício Toledo. História da Sociedade Brasileira. 13 ª Ed. Rio de Janeiro: Editora Ao Livro Técnico, 1996, p. 16.

nothing justifies a person seeing themselves as a friend of someone else's except for an anthropological explanation of the physiological and biased development of humans, as previously proclaimed by Pranchú regarding Antoine de Saint-Exupéri's and Nicolau Machiavelli's perspectives on their respective princes.

In his anthropological analysis, Pranchú makes a brief comparison of the physiological development of the Little Prince (Exupéri) and his transformation into the Prince (Machiavelli), establishing an inference between the distortion of a person and the exercise of public service.

Within the terms suggested by Pranchú, let's imagine that a citizen yearns to do public service (lato sensu), which is only possible through public entrance exams, elections, commissions, or other specific forms of entry into this type of career. An individual's personal intelligence before being a public agent, even with adequate academic instruction, offers practically no preparation for the turmoil and opportunities that the vicissitudes of public life will bring. Knowing that a person is honest or upright before entering this service is knowing merely that they are extremely good in terms of concepts, titles or personal indications, which could be interpreted as highly relevant public attribution. This is the figure of the "Little Prince" within public administration.

The literary work *The Little Prince* by Antoine de Saint-Exupéry is a fable that showcases several parables of moral judgments. Contrary to what many people think, *The Little Prince* is not aimed at children, but brings the message of childhood precisely as a way to awaken altruistic attitudes. The work contains metaphors that illustrate a virtuous child discovering the world in the middle of a desert, with mature reflections of what is right and wrong, as in the following example: "*It is much more difficult to judge yourself than to judge others. If you can judge yourself well, here true wisdom is found.*[42]" The most important message of this work, however, is on the importance of captivating someone: "*What is essential is invisible to the eyes. You become responsible, forever, for what you have captivated.*[43]" The importance of captivating lies in the responsibility of those who captivate, attributing a certain moral burden to people's actions.

---

[42] SAINT-EXUPÉRI, Antoine de. O Pequeno Príncipe. Rio de Janeiro: Editora AGIR, 1987, p. 41.
[43] SAINT-EXUPÉRI, Antoine de. Op. Cit., Pág. 74.

The public agent, in the role of Little Prince, is the virtuous professional who has caution when judging themselves and others, who is responsible for the public work they have captivated. In short, it is a virtue in view of what is public, even if it is due to a mandatory internship or the lack of stability in public employment. "Little Prince" public agents are governed by a series of ethical principles that guide them in their jobs, ensuring that, in many cases, no inhonorable acts or acts that harm morals are practiced.

In the temporary interregnum for the provision of public service, the "Little Prince" type of public agent can transform into the "Prince". Just as human beings suffer physiological development over the years, so do public agents. They grow and transmute from the "Little Prince" into the "Prince". This is not a normal transmutation, as in the experience of time that takes away the spontaneity of childhood and creates roots in the prudence of maturity. It is a transmutation vitiated by moral and ethical irregularities.

Now, let's turn to *The Prince*, a famous work by Nicolau Machiavelli. This political work has aroused controversies, with its share of problematic interpretations, debates, and certain obscure and paradoxical moments. The work raises fundamental issues such as the conquering of power and how to preserve it, how to create alliances, negotiate, and make political deals. It also exposes the relation between the State and the people, as well as corruption, nepotism, favoritism, and other, although no less important, secondary themes. The idea of the "Prince" is well known for its cynical amoralism translated as: "the ends justify the means", but let's see:

> *"Let the prince, therefore, keep his power; the means will always be judged honorable and praised by all, because the vulgar always let themselves be carried away by the appearance and the result of things; and in the world there is only the vulgar, the minority has no place when the majority has a foothold. Always triumph, no matter how, and you will always be right."*[44]

The public agent, in the role of "Prince", does not measure consequences in order to reach his main purpose, that is, to take advantage of public property. Thus, Machiavelli's realistic theory, which aimed at implementing a new order dominated by moral and physical freedom capable of stripping man's natural feelings of

---

[44] MAQUIAVEL, Nicolau. *O Príncipe: com notas de Napoleão Bonaparte.* 2 ª Ed. São Paulo: Editora Revista dos Tribunais, 1997, p. 115.

inferiority, is inadvertently utilized in order to benefit from public patrimony at society's expense. The deterioration eventually faced by public administration is caused by the deterioration of virtue into corruption, both by public agents and by part of the population.

The transformation invoked in this Pranchurian theory is the deterioration of public agents who, unsatisfied with what they have, procure their goods in the goods of the masses. It is this ambition which causes corruption and all other adjacent ills. The purpose of this theory, however, is not restricted to highlighting the deterioration of public agents, it also attempts to analyze the origin of this degenerative transformation.

The ingrained culture of favoritism, as demonstrated, explains part of the origin of the ethical and moral chaos which the country is experiencing, but it does not demonstrate its practical meaning. It is believed that one is ever satisfied with what one has, especially those who work for the public, and that it is their ambition the cause for corruption and other ethical and moral distortions, which spread like a cancer.

Brazilians, in terms of this Pranchurian theory and in view of this culture of favoritism, have begun to develop the spirit of discernment to try to survive and, in doing so, have yearned to always be more clever than their counterparts. This cleverness can be seen, for instance, when a driver decides to cut someone off by using the sidewalk or when they park in prohibited areas. It can also be seen when someone throws garbage in inappropriate places, when they cut lines if given the chance, when they buy products of dubious origins (such as contraband), when they vote for corrupt politicians who claim to have "accomplished" something, when they use illegal means to get access to electricity, when they enter a commercial establishment for the sole purpose of using its free internet, as well as several other acts that can even be configured as crimes.

The result is a distortion between self-interest and common interest, which for many is not a demerit. It was established as "Gerson's Law", named after a famous football player who once, in an advertisement, coined the well-known phrase "jeitinho brasileiro", or "the Brazilian way", which is the desire to always get an advantage in something. This method of creating innovative solutions or artifices is certainly of dubious ethical validity.

Well, in his anthropological analysis, Pranchú concluded that Brazilians became the Prince through truly mistaken teachings and that they necessarily deserve correction, even if only through a good beating. As occurred in the mistaken pedagogy of the past, Brazilians today must endure daily beatings to learn how to stop complaining about corruption, and correct themselves in their own personal, everyday corruptions. At the end of his anthropological homily on the ills of the Brazilians, Pranchú concluded with yet another pearl of wisdom:

> *"Cleverness without judgment is like saying that beauty is a matter of faith: the individual may even believe he is beautiful, but it will be quite difficult to convince others!"*

Thus said Pranchú!

"THE WORLD IS RUN BY THE EFFORTS OF THE INTELLIGENT, BUT IT IS THE INNOCENT SAGE WHO ENJOYS IT. LONG LIVE INNOCENCE AND PROMISCUITY!"

◇7

CONTEXTUALIZING THE DISCOURSE ON THE METHOD

He was a boy with sluggish features, caused by the harshness of the Brazilian northeast, more specifically the backlands of the state of Bahia, and his face reflected a deep attachment to his roots and the cultures of that same region. He was quite simple and had eyebrows with an air of humility to them, which was nothing more than pure modesty that revealed his intelligence and skills camouflaged in effortless and unpretentious acts. Naive and without malice, he restricted himself to making intelligible and profound ramblings about the simple things in life. He was methodical by nature, unattached by birth, and scholarly through hard work. Such was the incomparable Renezinho da *Bahêa*, a virtuous friend of the philosopher Pranchú.

Renezinho was a singer, composer and played the *zabumba* in a band called *Ki-Delícia* in Vitória da Conquista, Bahia[45]. The band specialized in the Brazilian style of *forró-axelizado*, a mixture that was quite *sui generis*[46], and they used to play axé[47] during the period of Carnaval[48] and *forró*[49] during the June festivities. The band never really took off and made only a few bucks, but Renezinho wasn't concerned about that at all. Although he had to make ends meet, he never let go of what he considered to be his life's toil.

Despite being endowed with extraordinary intelligence, Renezinho never used it effectively to get his own place in the sun. He said he was firm in his purposes and dedicated to his professional intent, even if it did not yield him anything promising. Renezinho would say that he was developing a scientific method that would establish some rules for guiding people's spirit. To develop this scientific method, he needed

---

[45] Vitória da Conquista is a city in Bahia, a Brazilian state in the Northeast of Brazil.

[46] In Brazil, Carnaval is a summer festival and June festivities occur during winter. In the United States, it would be as if the band played rock during half of the year and a completely different genre, like reggae, in the other half.

[47] Axé is a type of music from Bahia popularly played during Carnaval.

[48] A large Brazilian street party to celebrate Mardi-Gras.

[49] Forró is a type of music from the Northeast of Brazil and is popularly played during June festivities.

to let go of mundane things and use practical life as evidence. And that, he stated, was what justified his total devotion to the band Ki-Delícia.

This clever solution substantiated a life of partying committed only to hedonism. Pranchú immediately assumed that Renezinho had psychological problems and was numbed by this cheap philosophy to advocate for his life of debauchery. Renezinho, however, went on to further justify his choice from a philosophical point of view.

Renezinho said that he had been given his name in honor of the French philosopher René Descartes, who he had always been curious about when he was young. He had read all his namesake's written works and had immersed himself in the philosopher's thoughts, especially those extracted from *Discourse on the Method*, as if such thoughts were to simply become a part of his life. He had adopted the Cartesian method and defended the thesis that doubt was the first step towards any real knowledge. As if the act of doubting was indubitable itself, Rene actually began to get smarter! The only doubt he definitely didn't have, though, was related to his band Ki-Delícia. On this subject, René had absolutely no doubts!

Similarly, Renezinho also adopted the practical idea of the four basic Cartesian rules from his namesake's *Discourse on the Method*, which, according to him, could be applied in anyone's daily life. In a nutshell, these rules could be presented as follows:

1. *Rule of Clarity or Verification:* a person should only admit as true what is presented so clearly that there is no doubt about it.

2. *Rule of Analysis:* if someone finds it difficult to understand any kind of knowledge, it is necessary to divide this difficulty in as many parts as needed to arrive at clarity and thus solve the problem.

3. *Rule of Order or Synthesis:* thoughts must be conducted in order, starting with the simplest until the most complex. Deduction would be a way of expanding knowledge, from the simplest to the most composed.

4. *Rule of Enumeration:* revisions must be made as needed to guarantee that all elements of the analysis and deduction have been considered.

For Renezinho, the four Cartesian rules could be considered the *modus operandi* of reason and constituted the three elementary operations of the human mind: induction (which captures minimal realities), deduction (which groups observations and infers results), and enumeration (which reviews and re-elaborates concepts). Renezinho explained that following these rules minimized any kind of existential anguish he felt, even if he had to hold onto his glass of whiskey to do so.

Pranchú, however, had another inference for Renezinho, one with reasonable complexity to justify his "creative leisure" in the deepest sense, as told by Domenico De Masi[50]. The Cartesian method used by Renezinho served to account for the promiscuousness of his customs, as if his reason alone were self-sufficient. He would repeat his namesake's old mantra of *"Je pense, donc je suis"*, as if that gave him the authority of a reason that justified his hedonist way of life.

"But Renezinho, be a little more pragmatic and explain this to me: how does the Cartesian method work in your life?" challenged Pranchú.

"Meu rei (My king), it's simple. Playing and singing with Ki-Delicia is something so sublime for me that I have no doubt about carrying on with it. That is explained by the Rule of Clarity. If one day I do have doubts, I will share them with my fellow bandmates as stated in the Rule of Analysis. The idea will be to divide all my doubts and problems into various parts, so that each part becomes so small it disappears over time, which is what the Rule of Order brings us. With this strategy, we can always carry out this analysis so that other elements of deduction are also considered. Did you get it?"

"Oh my dear, party-loving friend, what I understand is that you are the most philosophical rogue I know! Now, getting you to do some laundry or lawn mowing would certainly be out of the question, wouldn't it? Not even if we combined all of Descartes' ontology and Locke and Hume's empiricism! Now, methodologically speaking, my friend, you are a bum of a superior kind, there's no doubt about that!"

---

[50] "He who is a master of the art of living makes little distinction between his work and his free time, between his mind and his body, between his education and his recreation, between his love and his religion. He has difficulty distinguishing one thing from another. He simply aims for excellence in whatever he does, leaving it to others to decide whether he is working or having fun. He believes he's always doing both at the same time"
MASI, Domenico de. O ócio criativo. Rio de Janeiro: Sextante, 2000, p. 328.

With that, Renezinho and Pranchú burst out laughing together. Regardless of any method for conducting reason, Renezinho learned that the problems life presents us with can be divided into several compartments in such a way that each one becomes smaller. His understanding of life was simple, light and pure, as there was no room for further complications, except for this skewed philosophy of his.

Unlike Renezinho's life though, many people's lives seem comfortable, with no major nuances that could take away their stability, but they're still full of doubts. Did I make the right choice? Is this the right way? Will it or will it not be? Anyway, who knows. But for Renezinho, doubt was the starting point to arrive at real knowledge, even though he had no doubts about his own desires. He used to say, paraphrasing the Brazilian composer Luiz Gonzaga:

"If I were born again and could choose, more than I am I would not want to be!"

He was a multifaceted Cartesian player of the zabumba[51], a true mugangueiro[52], immoral and with a vocation for naughtiness and teasing women, and none of these attributes defiled in any way his life in Bahêa, for he was too smart to understand that the grace of life was its simplicity, even if he needed to use philosophy to justify that simplicity.

And thus, with a spirit of Cartesianism and horseplay alongside the pretty brunettes of the region of Vitória da Conquista, Renezinho carried on with his life. Pranchú, on the other hand, thought about the paradigm established by Renezinho and, while trying to understand how such shallowness had reached actual depths, arrived at a Boolean conclusion about the Discourse on the Method a la Bahêa:

"The world is run by the efforts of the intelligent, but it is the innocent sage who enjoys it. Long live innocence and promiscuity!"

Thus said Pranchú!

---

[51] Zabumba: musical instrument from the Northeastern region of Brazil utilized to play *forró*.

[52] Mungangeiro: a person who has funny gestures and behaviour which are unusual and very expressive. The term comes from the Northeast of Brazil.

"ALL SIN THAT IS CONFESSED
HAS THE RIGHT TO BE
RENEWED. BUT DON'T BE
FOOLED. LIFE IS THE PROPERTY
OF GOD, WE ONLY GET TO
ENJOY IT."

THE WHOLE AND THE PART

"Pranchú, my friend, speaking rationally, the whole without the part is not the whole. Consequently, the part without the whole is not the part!"

"I know, Greg, but if the part makes up the whole by being the part, one can't say that is it the part - it's the whole!"

Their conversation carried on as if they had nothing better to do. At first sight, the dialogue could be understood as a discussion about something that was complete (the whole) or incomplete (the part). Actually, though, the talk was restricted to a more meaningful topic: friendship.

Pranchú had studied alongside Gregório in a Christian school in old Bahia[53], back in the 17th century, until the day Gregório moved temporarily to Portugal. His stay overseas was very long and his return to Bahia only occured in the second half of that century. Despite the fact that the two had always been friends, the distance kept them apart. Now Gregório was back and they would have the rest of the century to reconnect. That's just when their conversation continued.

Very well, their discussion was about the whole and the parts regarding friendship. For everything to be in order, the parts and the whole must also be in order. If any part wasn't good, then the whole wouldn't be good either. If the whole was good, so were all the parts. There is no way to prioritize a single part or to only focus on the whole and neglect the parts. One must look at the parts as a whole and treat the whole as the sum of its parts.

The two rambled on about friendship, with a vision that this would involve the parts and the whole. Friends are altruistic and should put themselves in each other's shoes, and also, consequently, at each other's side. A friendship in which

---

[53] Bahia, a Northern state of Brazil

one of the parts focuses only on itself, with no consideration for the other, is not a friendship. It will never be so because there is no such thing as a friendship with only one person and in which one individual decides what must be done. Money and other material goods cannot unite people in a friendship. There is no such thing as a self-benefitting friendship. There is no such thing as a friendship in which one of the parts buys the other part's company.

Friendship is comprehension and reciprocity, and what makes it beautiful is the fact that each of the parts shines with its own light, illuminating the way when one of the parts loses a bit of its brightness. Therefore, since the whole depends on the part, and the part depends on the whole, the totality of a friendship cannot be perfect because the parts that compose it are not. Evidently, there is no perfection in friendship, but there are ways to improve that which is not perfect in a friendship, in a way that can improve not only the whole, but also the parts. One cannot wish for the whole if one doesn't build a part of it. It was a discussion of pure altruism based on a moral construction about friendship.

In sincere friendships, Gregório thought, it was often necessary to transform that which was too crystalline into a kaleidoscope. Parting from a context connected to friendship, based on a conversation he had with old Pranchú, Gregório was able to absorb some premises that would launch his already well-known poetic feat. Thus, the whole and the part became simpler.

And so Gregório began working on what would be one of his main works of art, with the excuse that he would develop a theme related to the tearing down of a statue of Jesus whose only remaining part was an arm. The piece was simply entitled *"To the arms of the boy Jesus when it appeared"*:

The whole without the part, is not whole;
the part without the whole is not a part;
but if the part makes it whole, being a part,
let it not be said a part, being the whole.

In the whole Sacrament God is whole,
and exists as a whole in every part,
and though everywhere He is split apart,
in every part He is always whole.

Let not the arm of Jesus be a part,

for Jesus thus parted in his whole,
exists for his part in each part.

Not knowing itself part of the whole,
an arm which was taken as a part,
tells us the whole parts of the whole.[54]

When it was published, the poem thrilled audiences and was elevated to extraordinary heights. It was treated as a theological interpretation of the mystery of the Holy Trinity, in a way that illustrates how God is in the whole world, but also in all its parts. In this sense, God is the whole and Jesus the part, and one cannot exist without the other, as shown in the verses. God takes part in the whole Sacrament and is observed in any part, that is, in all things. Conscious of God's existence, one could open their eyes to see that in all parts of everything, one can find parts of the whole, that is, God.

Gregório, who had been nicknamed *"the mouth of hell"* because of his audacity and fervent criticisms towards the Catholic Church, and who had been attacked by Catholic priests many times, was now indubitably and divinely redeemed with this poem "To the arms of the boy Jesus when it appeared". The verses, however, were in fact a great paradox because the poet portrayed, as it were, how people are actually much more dependent on higher forces than on the Church itself and on themselves, in this case, on God.

What no one could imagine was that the whole and the parts emerged from a casual and greedless conversation, so much so that Pranchú never became upset with the fact that he was not given credit. As far as friendship is concerned, the lesson about the whole and the parts is timeless. If the parts are not improved and the whole continues to be seen as something singular and indivisible, there can never be harmony or even a well-working system, whether it is in a relationship, in a life goal, in a family, or in any other situation. The whole will never be whole without its parts, and the parts will never be a part without the whole.

---

[54] Poem translated by Mark A. Lokensgard. Available at: <http://www.antoniomiranda.com.br/Iberoamerica/brasil/gregorio_de_mattos.html#english>

Some time later, Gregório de Matos[55] met with Pranchú and, before his friend could speak, began:

"What good can being quiet do if he who is quiet cannot speak what he feels? One must feel what one speaks!"

Pranchú was quiet for a few minutes in front of Gregório because he knew that irony, a rare plant, only gave good fruit if it was showered with intelligence. With Gregório it was no different. Pranchú received those words as an apology and, in truth, they were. The philosopher then decided to contextualize the paradox that "the mouth of hell", his friend and poet, had experienced and replied calmly:

"All sin that is confessed has the right to be renewed. But don't be fooled. Life is the property of God, we only get to enjoy it."

Thus said Pranchú!!

---

[55] Gregório de Matos was an attorney and poet in Brazil when it was still Portuguese colony. He was one of the major baroque poets in Portugal and in Brazil, and was considered the most important satirical poet of the Portuguese language during the colonial period.

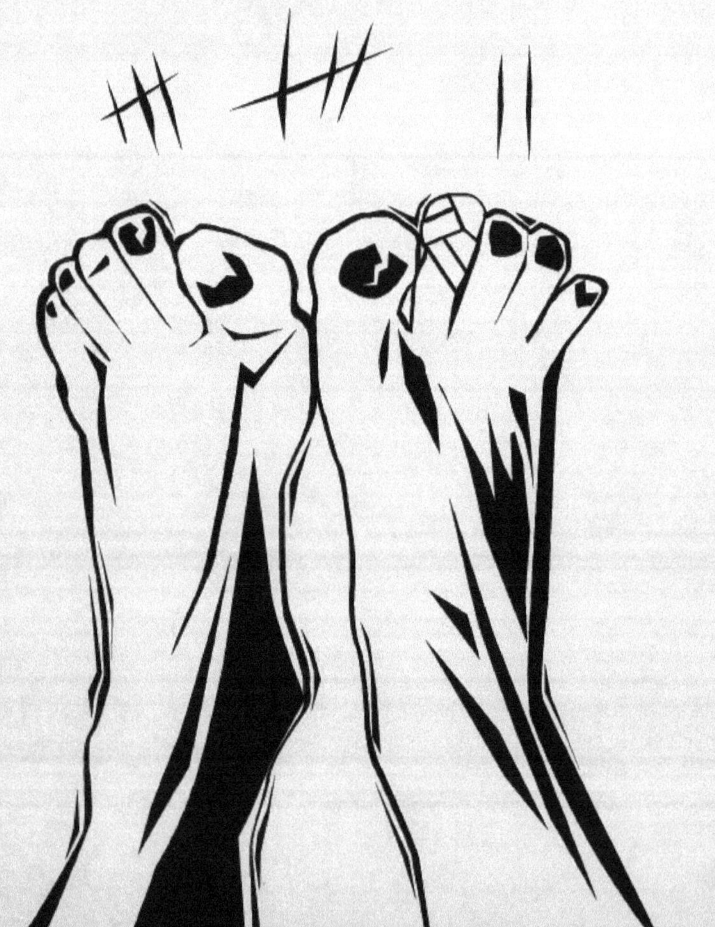

"LET EACH PERSON,
ACCORDING TO HOW MANY
TIMES THEY'VE TRIPPED,
MEASURE THE DEGREE OF
THEIR BLINDNESS."

CREATING THE SOCIAL CONTRACT

The course was called Civil Rights IV and was taught by Professor José de Farias Tavares. The students were sophomores and juniors, and the content was general contract theory. After numerous legal debates during the semester, Professor Tavares decided to draw pairs for the final project which would be worth the entire course grade. For the project, students would create contracts based on principles and other precepts they had discussed that semester and they would be evaluated not only based on the formality of their contracts, but most of all the content.

On that day, Pranchú arrived about five minutes late for class, which was the deadline established by the professor and enough time to make him furious. In sarcastic consideration, Professor Tavares did not include Pranchú's name in the pair draw, but instead personally selected our philosopher's companion for the project. Since it was an act of obvious retaliation to what was comprehended as extreme indiscipline, the professor indicated the most unbearable, aloof, and arrogant person he could find, one who had a distinctly blunt political posture. It was the indomitable Rousseau.

Rousseau was a Swiss youth who considered himself an intellectual, a spiritualist, and a defender of natural rights. This was reason enough to contribute to his status as a snobbish, spoiled, and caricatured foreigner. In college, Rousseau recounted some of the essays he had already written: *Discourse on Science and the Arts, New Heloise*, among others.

Pranchú and Rousseau decided to meet at the main library in the School of Law to begin their project. As there was no empathy between the two, Pranchú started up the dialogue:

"Let's avoid any more conflict, Rousseau. Let's be practical and extremely objective, since we don't have any time to lose. What shall be the object of our contract?"

"Pranchú, my intention is to develop a contract that will regulate someone's life when they pass from the natural state to the civil state."

"What do you mean 'my intention'? This is pair work, my friend! And also, what the hell is this contractual object you're talking about?"

"My friend, it is a contract related to life or death, and individual slavery. Why would a person born free become a slave?"

"Hold on! I think you might be confusing the courses. We studied sociology and philosophy last year! Now, our course is about contracts. Have you forgotten that?"

"But that is exactly what I'm going to write about. And you? What kind of contract do you have in mind?"

"I'm not sure, I thought about writing a contract on leases with resolute clauses."

"Leases with resolute clauses? Well, wouldn't that be a perpetuate contract about public and private land?"

"Well done, Rousseau, at least you know what the contract means, even if you are responding to me with a question."

"Pranchú, I am not going to write a contract in which the copyholder becomes a slave in exchange for subsistence."

"But didn't you just tell me you'd like to write about slavery."

"Not that kind of slavery. I want to write about the slavery that bases itself on life or death and that creates a vicious cycle…"

Interrupting Rousseau, Pranchú tried to end the discussion:

"All right, well let's leave slavery aside and let's focus on our contract. With no philosophical ramblings, please. So, what should be the objective of our contract?"

"My contract would only have one clause: the alienation of all individuals to make them equal."

"Listen, Rousseau, I apologize in advance for what I'm going to say but – fuck you! I'm going to tell you something that many of our classmates would like to tell you: you are an insufferable fellow who has no vocation for the juridical world. Why don't you try philosophy, sociology, gastronomy, or even ballet? Can you see the secretary from here? Just walk over there and ask to be transferred!"

Surprised by that attitude of Pranchú's, especially because no one had ever given him a reality check, Rousseau replied resignedly:

"Actually, I've already thought about transferring. I haven't done it yet because I'm trying to find myself here in Law studies."

"Sure, but the problem is that Law studies doesn't want to find you at all. You're completely lost, more than a harlot's child on Fathers' Day! Now, you do have some good ideas, but you're off-track. Think of it like this - if '*a person is born good and society corrupts them*', then maybe you might be a little corrupted."

Staring blankly and holding his chin with one hand, Rousseau reiterated Pranchú's words:

"'*A person is born good and society corrupts them*.' Doesn't that have some considerable depth to it? It's exactly what ratifies the social pact I intend to develop further in the rough draft of an essay I've been writing for a few years now."

"Oh, Rousseau, you want to write a 'social contract', which is inherently political, in a Civil Rights course? Don't you think that's too much shit for such a small bowl?"

"That's right, Pranchú. I want to write about a 'social contract'. That's my insight!"

"'Insight' is a thing of leftist enlightenments! You're turning into Voltaire!"

"Oh no, please, don't compare me to that unqualified fellow, Pranchú!"

"So be a man, Rousseau! Find your way and write about your trip. It will be hilarious: '*Daydreams of a lonely wanderer*'".

After this episode, Rousseau took Pranchú's advice and went on his philosophical crusade. He was nowhere to be seen, to the joy of his classmates.

Pranchú, however, saw himself at a huge disadvantage in that moment since his partnership fell through. This certainly would not be well received by the professor and, worst of all, the project was due the following day.

When Professor Tavares arrived in class the next day, he noticed that all the students were there, with the exception of Rousseau, whose presence was generally notorious because he used to sit opposite the professor with that air of superiority and petulence. It didn't take long for the professor to ask:

"Pranchú, come forward and explain, first of all, your classmate's absence on the day your project is due and, if there even is a justification, present your own work."

Pranchú went to the center of the class and began his presentation:

"'*Rebus sic stantibus*', an old Latin term applied in contractual clauses, is the basis for a so-called 'theory of the unforeseen', which is an exception to the rule of 'pacta sunt servanda', or the principle of a contract's obligatory force. 'Rebus sic stantibus' consists in the acknowledgment that new events, whether foreseen or not by the parts, or even attributed to them, have an impact on the execution of contracts and authorize revisions to make adjustments according to the supervenient circumstances."

"Ok, Pranchú, but what does that have to do with Rousseau's absence?"

"Very well, noble professor. We had a non-verbal contract in which Rousseau and I would present a contract based on the principles and other precepts we discussed during the course. However, not only did Mr. Jean-Jacques Rousseau stop collaborating on this project about contracts, but he also transferred from Law to another major, abandoning the course. Ergo, 'rebus sic stantibus' shall be used in my contractual consideration and therefore there are readjustments to be made regarding the demands of my presentation."

"Alright, Pranchú, you've defended it well. And what is the contract you'll present to us?"

"A contract on leases with resolute clauses."

"And what's the epistemological basis for your contract, Pranchú?"

"Well, the structural paradigms of my contract rest exactly on the last colloquium I had with Rousseau before he gave up studying Law":

"Let each person, according to how many times they've tripped, measure the degree of their blindness."

-A+!

Thus said Pranchú!

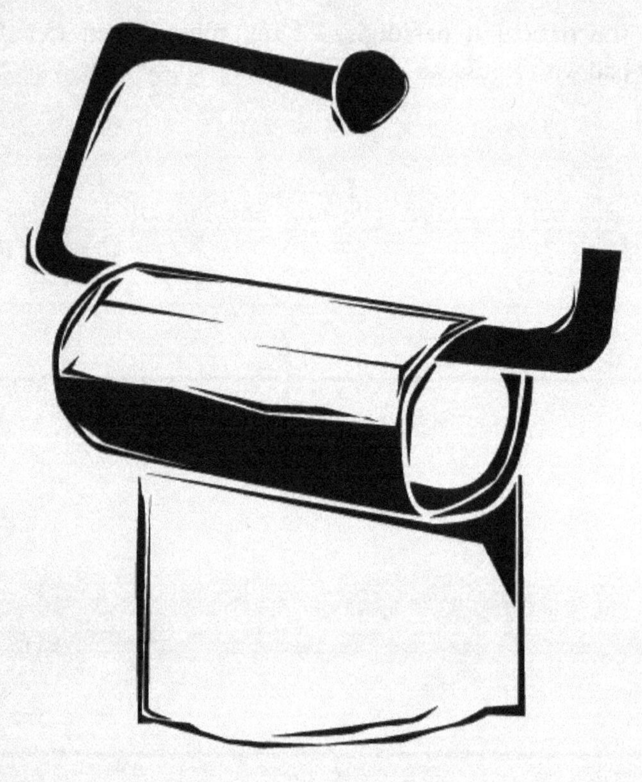

"BEFORE YOU SPEAK, LISTEN.
BEFORE YOU ACT, THINK.
BEFORE YOU GIVE UP, TRY.
BEFORE YOU SHIT, MAKE SURE
THERE IS PAPER!"

10 ◈

HEGEL'S DIALECTICS ACCORDING TO PRANCHÚ

Pranchú, a tenured Philosophy professor at the *Bodacious Philosophy University* (UNIBODE) in the countryside of Texas, gave lectures on Dialectics to students in their senior year. The professor tried to simplify the topic, but he always came up against the natural difficulty of comprehending dialectics as an infinite cycle of mutations, as well as the usual commotion among the students. Pranchú explained:

"The development of scientific thought, especially in the history of Physics, has demonstrated that scientific knowledge is in constant evolution and change. Thus, to analyse knowledge based on a single and atemporal philosophical system, in light of the dynamic nature of the actions and practices to which science subjects itself, is to delineate an oversimplified trajectory of the evolution of ideas, concepts, and scientific theories. Regarding this topic, Gaston Bachelard[56], a contemporary French philosopher, has criticized the traditional, empirical-inductivist image of science. Besides his concerns, there's also the formation of the scientific spirit which is not Hermetic."

"Professor, what do you mean by 'Hermetic'?" asked the student in the first row.

"According to Bachelard, one cannot consider a closed image of science, reflected in a single epistemological concept which universally describes the genesis and development of scientific thought. A 'progressive' or 'open' standpoint, based on what Bachelard denominates as 'dialectics', must permeate the vision of contemporary science. Bachelard highlights that 'in the physical sciences, rational organization and experience are in constant cooperation'. Hence, it is a fallacious ideal to think of science only in terms of rationalist doctrine or an empirical thesis

---

[56] BACHELARD, Gaston. *A Formação do Espírito Científico*. Rio de Janeiro: Contraponto, 1999.

since, according to Bachelard, both are necessarily complementary."

The lecture seemed to be going at an intellectually reasonable rate when suddenly one of the students from the back of the class, casually dressed in an abadá[57] with matching Havaiana flip flops[58], raised his hands and asked:

"But professor, in an objective sense, what the hell is 'dialectics'?"

With the patience of a Benedictine monk, Pranchú replied.

"According to the common lexis, dialectics is the art of dialogue. In a very general sense, it's opposition or conflict which originates in contradiction between theoretical principles and empirical phenomena. Over time, dialectics became the art of - in dialogue - demonstrating a thesis with an argument capable of clearly defining and distinguishing concepts involved in a discussion."

Is that so? I didn't even know that existed!" cried the student. The professor continued.

"There are various embryonic concepts of dialectics, such as the dialectic methods of Platonism, Aristotelism, Kantism, Hegelianism, Marxism, among others. The modern sense of dialectics is that it's 'the way in which we consider the contradictions of reality, or the way in which we comprehend reality as essentially contradictory and in permanent transformation'. Dialectics is a way of establishing patterns of scientific transformation employing discussions and the use of logical arguments."

Another student from the back row, now showing reasonable interest in the lesson, asked:

"But how is that done in a practical way? That is, if one can even practice dialectics!"

"Dialectics is a construction of thought which is developed when there's a rupture of previous thoughts and a brand new structure in way of thinking. In this case, dialectics is constituted with the aid of three methods substantiated in a

---

[57] Abadá is a loose-fitting, casual t-shirt famously used in Brazilian Carnaval festivities.
[58] Havaiana flip flops are a trademark of a relaxed, Brazilian lifestyle.

syllogism entitled 'thesis, antithesis, and synthesis'. The thesis is the statement or the initially given situation. The antithesis is the opposition of the thesis. The synthesis comes from the conflict between the thesis and the antithesis, and it's a new situation resulting from that clash. In other words, it is the situation which comes from a paradigm rupture in a discussion. Consequently, the synthesis becomes a new thesis, which will eventually be contrasted with a new antithesis and result in a new synthesis. It's a cyclical process in the structuring of thought."

"Ok, I think I get it. But, so what? How can we put that into practice? asked the student."

"As an object of thought structuring, dialectics can be understood when it is applied in a practical case of discussion in an everyday scenario. For instance, we can observe dialectics in nature - the passing of the days, the changing of the seasons, the transformation of all that surrounds us. One example is a caterpillar (thesis), a cocoon (antithesis), and a butterfly (synthesis). Nature works in cycles, such as yesterday, today, and tomorrow, and that is also how species perpetuate in their generations - life (growing up), death (aging), and rebirth (fruit, children), or thesis, antithesis, and synthesis. Here's another example - a chair is made of wood (thesis), the chair is not only made of wood (antithesis), the chair is a product of human work with the aid of instruments (synthesis). Synthesis is constituted when a new thesis must be developed, therefore it is not possible to speak of 'evolution' without dialectics."

After the professor's explanation, a student from the middle of the class thought out loud:

"How psychedelic! Too much of a high with not enough weed."

Pretending not to understand the comment, Pranchú asked:

"What's that?"

"Oh, nothing, professor - just a dialectic thought!"

At that moment, when the discussion had been leaning towards the profound, a mysterious figure entered the classroom, one that had never even passed by that door before. A girl sat down and, before anyone could even muster a thought, raised her hand and said out loud:

“Professor, I need to speak with you about my absences.”

“I apologize for not identifying you, what is your grace?”

“Hegeliana Moore”.

Upon hearing that name, the professor remembered that this young lady had already failed due to absences about four months earlier, because she had not been to a single class. In an attempt to assuage the situation, the professor said:

“Of course, we can talk during the break.”

The student, however, awkwardly and unintentionally insisted:

“No, I wish to discuss this here and now!”

Pranchú, who didn't care for any type of awkward situation, accepted the student's request.

“Very well, how may I help you?”

“Sir, I'd like you to review the days I missed class.”

“Which missed days, dear? You were simply not present in my class.”

“Well, isn't missing days and not being present the same thing? she sarcastically asked.”

“Oh no, my dear. As I said, you were simply not present in class. But you were certainly not missed in class any day! Now, please, see yourself out.”

The students watched that scene with perplexion. They were stunned with the girl's lack of manners and with the professor's wit and how he was able to handle the situation wisely and calmly. As soon as the student had left, the professor asked:

“Did you comprehend how dialectics works in a practical way?”

The students didn't answer. The silence that echoed throughout the classroom had an air of epiphany, so the professor seized the opportunity.

“The young lady who entered our classroom wanted to discuss the days she had missed in class. What does that represent in dialectical thought?"

Some students answered under their breath:

"The thesis."

"And then I replied that she was simply not present in my class. What does that represent in dialectical thought?"

"The antithesis" replied a student, with a little more enthusiasm.

"And what could be the synthesis?" Asked the professor. After a few seconds, when no one had said anything, the professor answered himself.

"The synthesis is this - not being present does not mean being missed. Notice how the clash of understanding, in this case, ends with the rupture of an initially peaceful perception (thesis), which generated the final position (synthesis) and allowed us to understand that being present and being missed are different. The dialectics, however, does not end with the overlap of thesis, antithesis, and synthesis. It is renovated every time the argumentative method is presented in the solution of controversial issues. It's important to clarify that dialectics is not a simple addition of the properties of two opposing things, as in a simple mixture of opposites, but it is an autodynamic reformulation of knowledge."

Still confused but now immersed in the concept of dialects, the students finally gave in to the professor's cunning and his lessons, which were absorbed like water in dry land. Amid the collective catharsis, a student from the back row whose grasp was a bit more profound, asked:

"Professor, can we call this an example of Hegel's dialectics[59]?"

"Of course, literally!"

"And how can we act dialectically in our daily lives without overdoing it, but also without hesitating?"

---

[59] Hegeliana era o nome da aluna que criou a ingresia com o mestre e também, coincidentemente, era o nome do método dialético criado por Georg Wilhelm Friedrich Hegel (Dialética Hegeliana), baseado no silogismo: tese, antítese e síntese.

"My dear, we must simply follow the *'before' rule.*"

"*'Before'?* What do you mean?" asked the pupil.

Now in sermon-form, Pranchú stated:

Before you speak, listen.

Before you act, think.

Before you give up, try.

Before you shit, make sure there is paper!

Thus said Pranchú!

"FOR THE FELLOW WHO IS BAD AT FUCKING, EVEN THE BALLSACK GETS IN THE WAY!"

11

CHALAÇA AND MEN'S THREE SOUNDS

Since ancient times, onomatopoeia has always been man's most used feminine noun, in the most masculine sense of the word. Even without knowing it, men use onomatopoeia as a means to heal hardships and to obscure their most intrinsic aspirations and desires. Onomatopoeia, in fact, was the object of some profound reflections in the History of Brazil, especially during the declaration of our independence.

According to the classical historiography of Brazil, on September 7, 1822, on the banks of the Ipiranga stream, the then Regent Prince of Brazil and future emperor Don Pedro I, Don Pedro de Alcântara de Bragança, supposedly declared to his entourage the words "Independence or Death!" This is the part that everyone knows, but there are other parts embedded in our DNA and we, as Brazilians, make tremendous efforts to ignore them.

Don Pedro I's entourage had an unusual figure, whose Christian name was Francisco Gomes da Silva but who was also known as Chalaça. According to the historian Assis Cintra, this figure was the bastard son of the Viscount of Vila Nova da Rainha and a poor 19-year-old village girl who worked as a handmaiden for the Viscount's family. When Don João VI and the royal family came to Brazil in 1808, Chalaça was ordained an honorary servant of the Imperial Palace.

According to classic historiography, Chalaça had a *"loud, extravagant, insolent, and dissipated"*[60] character. From a simple private servant of the Palace, he was promoted by Emperor Don João VI to Assistant of the Guard of Honor and to the emperor's Private Secretary. It's possible to say without exaggeration that Chalaca's ascendance took over the emperor's spirit in such a way that the servant shared supreme authority with his master. Chalaça was also gifted with an absurdly keen intelligence and, after several conflicts within the royal family, he started to act as cabinet-officer, secretary, scribe, confessor, and advisor to D. Pedro I, then Regent Prince of Brazil.

---

[60] ARMITAGE, João. História do Brasil. São Paulo: Melhoramentos, 1977, p. 111.

The institutional role Chalaça had allowed for a thin bridge to friendship, which was why he started to assume a very unusual position before Don Pedro I: the role of Advisor of Licentious Affairs (ALA), that is, an advisor of whoring! Chalaça, now Counselor Gomes, was a forty-year-old subject and partner of the young Don Pedro I in his incursions to the brothels of the time, known for his sagacity and virtuosity in dealing with women, subsidizing the Regent Prince in his treatment of all types of youths. The Prince's regency with Chalaça was aimed at mere libertinism and light naughtiness, or the regency of institutionalized whoring.

Their most recent historical tales demonstrate that Chalaça was also very perceptive when it came to money, becoming allies, in politics and in the alcove, with even the devil himself to get what he wanted. The later memoirs published by Counselor Gomes himself portray that he was also fond of flattery and brownosery, other reasons for his success.

In his selfless and intriguing journey with Emperor Don Pedro I, Chalaça developed theses and antitheses that would one day be inserted in the DNA of Brazilian men, as previously explained. Based on the theory of the three sounds, inspired by El hombre y las cosas tríplices and mentioned by the chronicler José Roberto Torero, Counselor Gomes created a philosophical saying fundamented on three noises that would eventually become a moral aphorism for Brazilian males:

"Everything that a man seeks in the course of his experience are three sounds. Not two and never four. These are: the whisper of women, the clink of coins, and the roar of applause. No man will be able to consider himself fully satisfied - even though he may pretend he does not miss them, like some devotees do - if, at least once in his life, he has not come in contact with them."[61]

These are three axiological truths, metonymically formulated, whose conclusions have been incorporated into the psyche of the Brazilian male, not considering adjectives or derivations of postmodern concepts of metrosexuality or the like. In other words, the application of these truths leaves no margin for those who are unsure of their own masculinity.

---

[61] TORERO, José Roberto. *Galantes memórias e admiráveis aventuras do virtuoso conselheiro Gomes, O chalaça.* Rio de Janeiro: Objetiva, 2001, p. 92.

The three sounds of men, thought up by a deviant yet highly qualified man himself, refer to the objectives meticulously pursued by the typical Brazilian male, whether he's at a refined restaurant with a girl or at a celebration of Carnaval, where no one belongs to anyone. All that matters, according to Chalaça, is man's contemplation of the three sounds during the course of his existence.

Henceforth, no man will be fully realized if he does not hear the whispers of women, in the plural form, during his brief passage on Earth. Perhaps it is this sound that resembles the earthquakes, tidal waves or tsunamis which provoke men to walk endless miles in the search of a woman. No man cuts his hair, shaves, puts on perfume or grooms himself if not for the sake of a beautiful girl. According to Counselor Gomes, it is women and their whispers that move the world.

Likewise, according to Chalaça, there is no way to be a fully satisfied man without the onomatopoeia which comes from the clink of coins. It is, as the aforementioned metaphor connotes, the satisfaction a man gets from financial accomplishments and successes. There is no way, after all, to be a playboy without if you can't pay. There are those who say that the need for this onomatopoeia arises precisely so that a man can achieve the first sound, whispers of women, since courting a lady, whether in a restaurant or brothel, requires financial resources.

The last sound, stated Chalaça, would be the roar of applause, which represents the recognition or praise bestowed on a man. It is the exaltation of virtues, the contemplation of something that differentiates one man from another. There are those who say that this onomatopoeia is also meant to contemplate the first sound, the whispers of women, since no man seeks to be virtuous in something just for the joy of it. For example, it is clear that a man goes to a gym to work out not only because of his health, but also to show himself off to women. A simple conclusion, thus, can be extracted here: exercising objectifies women!

In the same way that a doctrine composes a philosophical system, which incorporates knowledge to men over the years, the theory of the three sounds created by Counselor Gomes has been embedded in the deoxyribonucleic acid of the Brazilian man and stigmatized in various circumstances, deals, facts, events, conditions or circumstances.

Football and soccer, for example, is considered a national passion precisely because it is the most sincere expression of the perfect search for the three sounds: *the whisper of women, the clinking of coins, and the roar of applause.* Who has never had a childhood dream of being a football player and repeatedly listening to these three sounds?

Another example is beer. Tasting beer is also a search for the three sounds of a man, even if it is an ephemeral search. The guy who goes to the bar, drinks beer and gets drunk, even without dignity, will certainly be a victim of the breathtaking sensation of the three sounds, after all, every drunk is *rich, handsome, and jeweled!* The guy starts to talk loudly, thinking that all women are flirting with him, and pays a lot for his beer, and also for his friends'.

Another very common example can be seen in business. He who succeeds in business is also on a perfect search for the three sounds, provided he is indeed a man. In Brazil, there is a very curious mantra known by successful entrepreneurs: when one becomes a millionaire, they like to show off! As far as these successful entrepreneurs are concerned, it is also possible to notice their famous exchange of a woman in her sixties for one in her thirties, the infamous "female upgrade". It is common to see an elderly millionaire showing off and holding his granddaughter's, I mean his new wife's, hand.

Well, the theory of the three sounds, created by a rustic, crude, and systematic subject, as they say in Goiás[62], is part of the epidermis of the Brazilian macho-man and is the object of a legacy that has been passed down from generation to generation. It is renewed each day by a formula whose objective is to stay eternally relevant despite new fashions such as metrossexuality and other vanities typical of the female gender. The theory of the three sounds has evident axiological basis in the Pranchurian scrolls as far as women are concerned, after all, as the philosopher would say, "women love men who have qualities that are the direct opposite of their faults."

If Chalaça were alive, he would certainly update the three sound theory to encompass all the feelings that human beings have for one another, regardless of gender, race, religion, political opinion, age, and other differences that do not matter. The three sounds would go through a major update to break through all kinds of prejudice today. The three sounds of life, or the onomatopoeia of life, would now be: the whispers of love, the clinks of coins, and the roar of applause.

---

[62] A Brazilian state.

The person who has never sought the three sounds Chalaça explained is certainly marked by nature and possibly keeps themselves from the joys of life. It is as if the they have not yet discovered themselves or, as Master Pranchú said during the Phoenecian invasion of São José da Lagoa Tapada:

"For the fellow who is bad at fucking, even the ballsack gets in the way!"

Thus said Pranchú!

"WHY TAKE LIFE SO
SERIOUSLY IF TO GET
HERE SOMEONE MUST GET
FUCKED?"

12

THE BROTHERS GRIMM AND THE HOLLYWOOD CIGARETTE

In his linguistic and poetic journey, Pranchú made great friends, among them were Jacob and Wilhelm. Also known as the Brothers Grimm, they were German scholars, linguists, and writers who dedicated their lives to writing children's fables which became famous worldwide. Some of their titles included *Hansel and Gretel, Snow White, Rapunzel, Tom Thumb*, and many more.

When they were in the final years of college, Jacob and Willhelm had a casual and quick meeting with Pranchú. Though short, their encounter was an opportunity for mutual deference. Pranchú and the Grimm brothers had a long conversation about literature and poetry, in particular on the creative process. They exchanged ideas about the object of each piece of writing and about the methodology for concluding their works.

The Grimm brothers mentioned that their stories emerged from intertextuality, that is, inspired by tall tales told by folks from various regions. The brothers collected information about certain facts, many times considered less important because of their unrealistic origins, and then transformed those facts into stories with mostly happy endings.

Pranchú, on the other hand, explained that his creative process was determined by moments of epiphany, especially when he was in an inebrious state. Pranchú said he didn't write while drunk, but that his insights emerged from a moment of ecstasy, which was generally caused by booze. He called it the ethylic process.

Upon hearing Pranchú's explanations, Jacob, the most introspective of the brothers, had doubts regarding the quality of the pranchurian writings which resulted from the philosopher's creative process. Pranchú explained that his creative process was different from the brothers', but not any less efficient, since the remote origin of each piece was part of each individual's subconsciousness and all they needed to know was how to arouse it. Actually, explained Pranchú, only 1% of the process was inspiration. The other 99% were transpiration.

Considering the philosopher's explanation and taking the opportunity as a moment to exercise their minds, Jacob had a proposition for Pranchú - the philosopher would imagine a proper Grimm brothers' childhood fable and then narrate it. Pranchú felt challenged and therefore replied with a counterproposition - he asked the brothers for a pen, a piece of paper, and only ten minutes. When the time was up, despite not having a single sip of alcohol, Pranchú presented his short, yet-to-be-entitled parable:

"We are always out of money! Don't you think so?"

"Yeah, we never have money for anything and yet mother doesn't save at all!"

"True! Take her famous cigarette vice, for example! Why can't she stop smoking and save up to buy milk? You know, milk is so expensive nowadays!"

"And the worst part is that there is nothing we can do - we can't cry, or scream, or even go on a hunger strike. She only listens to the cigarettes."

"Remember when both of us couldn't sleep one night because of so much tossing and turning? She didn't sleep either. God, it seemed like one of those glory days, or generational battles."

"Right. But in the end, she won. And to relax? Cigarette smoke right in our faces."

"I think I'm gonna have a serious conversation with her tonight or at least I'll make her think about everything."

"There's no way, brother! Remember when she drank so much whisky that she threw up all of her lunch? I have never been so sick in my entire life. The smell still makes me nauseous. And you know what she did after vomiting? She lit up a cigarette to calm herself down."

"How gross! I do remember. That smell stayed in the room for a while."

"You know what's worse? Today, I kind of like the smell of cigarette smoke! It's like smelling that old bedsheet of ours, the one with some threads coming undone? We used to run our noses on those threads and feel a tickle in our nostrils. I still do it when mom gets that old bedsheet."

"I kind of like the smell, too. I really hate smoke in my face, though. It's worse than when someone spits on you!"

"That's true! Getting smoke blown on your face is the worst. And sometimes you can't even run!"

"You know, I also don't understand why mom holds her cigarette the way she does, so delicately. She's masterfully subtle, with legs strategically crossed and an air of arrogance on her face. I've never really noticed it in other people, but do you think they also get this air of overconfidence when they smoke?"

"I'm not sure, I've never paid attention either! But now that you've mentioned it, I think mother is more delicate with her cigarette than our father. One time, I overheard a conversation she had with a friend who was in the middle of a divorce, and mother told her: 'men are like cigarettes, when they've given you everything they had and there's nothing left, throw them away!' I didn't understand what she meant by that, but I don't think it was a good thing."

"I don't know if mother is a good advice giver, but what I do know is that she keeps her cigarettes safe as if they were sacred. It's a pity, because she didn't do the same even with our little sister's photos."

"Brother, can you see what I see?"

"Smoke in my face? Not again!"

"Run, little brother, go anywhere else!"

"I'm going to hide behind the lungs."

"Are you crazy? The lungs are full of gross, black ashes that can stain your hands."

"I'll find a spot in the liver, then."

"What liver? Did you forget that last week mom's whiskey ate up half her liver? She doesn't even know yet. Be quiet and hide somewhere else."

"Alright. But not the intestine, because it's full of shit."

"Shut up and hide behind the pancreas!"

"I can't! There's a huge seed there, the size of a tangerine. I'm not going there!"

"Stay close to the ribs then, and don't move!"

"I would, but the ribs have shrunken so much because of her smoking that my legs can't fit!"

"You're a really dumb twin brother, you know!"

"Oh really, smart aleck, where are you going to hide?"

"I'm not. I'm enjoying this smell of Hollywoodian nicotine - it's a hit! My head is going crazy!"

"Well, alright, since you're so much smarter than me, where should I hide?"

"I don't know! Figure it out! You're such a pain in the ass!"

"Oh no, not there, not again!"

When they had finished reading the pranchurian parable, the Grimm brothers were quite surprised by the author's wit, especially because the narrative was truly similar to the brothers' lives. Though they weren't twins, as told in the tale, their real mother did in fact smoke. Jacob became very curious and asked Pranchú a question:

"But, how did you have this insight without that moment of ecstasy you mentioned before?"

"Well, Jacob, when someone challenges us, that becomes in itself a moment of ecstasy which can spark insight!"

"Alright, Pranchú. But why this parable?"

"I'm not sure, Jacob, it just came to mind! In most of the Grimm brothers' tales, there are characters such as dragons, wolves, monsters, witches, and other folkloric creations. They probably came from tragic stories that were passed down generations until they reached you brothers, and then were altered to have happy, lighter endings for children and teenagers. Perhaps this narrative I created can inspire you to write another tale."

"Well what kind of tale can one get from the ashes of a cigarette, Pranchú?"

"I don't know, maybe a story about a maiden who accumulates a lot of ashes? Who knows! Maybe this woman works with cinders somewhere? Her story could translate the human psyche's natural desire for recognition and for being elevated to superior existences."

Wilhelm, who had been a silent participant in the discussion, was writing down all the details of the profound conversation, almost as if in a trance. This deep moment of intertextual development was the brothers' trademark. His hands now gestured chaotically, his body language was agitated as he mumbled under his voice:

"Cinders Ella...Cinder-Ella...Cinderella!"

Pranchú joked:

"Ella? All yours, Wilhelm!"

Jacob, who was still curious about Pranchú's cleverness, decided to ask him an unusual question:

"Pranchú, what was that Hollywodian cigarette you mentioned in the story?"

"I have no idea, I only created it now! Coming from you, though, I think it would be a hit!"

And that's how Pranchú, on a typical afternoon with the Brothers Grimm, suggested the creation of two of their most successful works: *Cinderella*[63] and the

---

[63] The title Cinderella originates from the combination of the word cinder (meaning "ash" or "a piece of burned coal or wood") and the feminine suffix -ella, and is adapted from the Italian word "*Cenerentola*" (cenere means is the color grey in Italian).

Hollywood Cigarette. Whether from good to bad or bad to good, the important thing was being able to extract a life lesson from a simple tale, removing the heavy burden of the ashes, or cinders, and contextualizing life's choices. After all, as old Pranchú would say:

"Why take life so seriously if to get here someone must get fucked?"

Thus said Pranchú!

"NO IDEA IS USELESS OR
IDIOTIC. THE BEST WAY TO
HAVE A GOOD IDEA IS TO HAVE
MANY IDEAS, EVEN USELESS
AND IDIOTIC ONES!"

13

THE BROTHERS KARAOFMYEGGS: A LESSON ABOUT IDEAS

The word "idea" comes from the Greek *idea* ou *eidea*, whose etymological root is *eidos*, or image. There have been frequent philosophical discussions about the term (Plato, Aristotles, Hobbes, Descartes, Locke, Hume, Kant, Hegel, and others), but its dictionary definition conceptualizes the term idea as a mental representation of something that is concrete, abstract, or chimerical, and other similar concepts. An idea can both be something or nothing at all, according to the circumstances. To Pranchú, however, who paraphrased Voltaire, "ideas are like beards - a man only has one when it grows." It was based on this conception that Pranchú planted an attractive idea and only reaped indignation. What happened, though, did not and could not hinder his imagination, which was like a cauldron boiling up new ideas.

Very well, around the year 1865, Pranchú was awarded a Rotary Club scholarship to participate in an exchange program at the University of St. Petersburg, located in an icy, czarist Russia. Upon his arrival, Pranchú was directed to a student dormitory where he would share a room with two brothers, Ivan and Alyocha. The duo welcomed Pranchú and seemed to be good people despite often bringing up their family issues.

Pranchú's routine included daily visits to the University of St. Petersburg, where he had made various Russian friends due especially to an interest in vodka and *caipirinha made in Paraíba*[64]. Alcohol, after all, does have great benefits on the body in a cold environment. His Russians friends, it turns out, were mad for the *pinga*[65] from Paraíba, and it was between drinks one day that Pranchú met the pristine fellow Fyodor, a wannabe author who wandered around the campus. Fyodor was also a great fan of liquor and the commotion that comes from drinking and

---

[64] Paraíba is a Brazilian state located in the Northeastern region of the country.
[65] This is a typical Brazilian liquor extracted, by fermentation and distillation, from the sugar cane molasses.

always seemed to be thirsty, like someone who has just returned from exile. Pranchú and Fyodor soon found they had a lot in common and became close friends and partners in the art of drinking until becoming epitleptic or, as Freud would say, until they were hysteriallically ill!

As he made his way back to the dorm in the freezing cold one night, Pranchú met Ivan and Alyocha, who were lamenting about their family troubles. Their family was a mess! The father, also named Fyodor, a common name at the time, was a crook who had abandoned his children for a carefree life of parties. They also had an older brother, the hellish Dmitri, a really problematic soldier who thought himself to be a motherfucking intergalactic type. Ivan and Alyocha talked for a while, explaining that Fyodor and Dmitri, father and son, had been fighting over the same woman, who, in turn, seemed to be a hooker. Pranchú replied that where he came from, women didn't seem to be hookers, they either were or weren't. The brothers' laments went on throughout the night.

Pranchu's daily routine continued so during all his time in Russia. Daytime meant studying, philosophizing, and drinking vodka with college friends, including the philosopher and boozer Fyodor, to whom Pranchú told all the stories about his roommates Ivan and Alyocha. They talked about theology and psychology, but also, and especially, about existentialism. Vodka and existentialism. They drank until they kissed the ground, showing off their passion to do good on this earth. At night, when Pranchú reached his dorm room, he was forced to listen to his roommates' endless laments.

This melancholy routine every night was making Pranchú feel impatient and suffocated. He told Fyodor that his nightlife was now simultaneously a crime and a punishment, with no judicial rights. Fydor would scratch his chin and say:

"You know, that would make a good tile for a book, Pranchú!"

And Pranchú would reply:

"Oh, Fyodor, how are 'crime and punishment' good terms to use for a title? A good book title would actually be something like 'O Muído dos Irmãos da Kara dos Meus Ovos (Karaofmyeggs)![66]", which is a nice way to mention the brothers hardships.

The two friends would laugh uncontrollably and then drink until they were epileptic. They would discuss existentialism once again and, in this case, how the existentialism of a hooker could ruin a family!

One night, when Pranchú arrived at his dorm room he found Alyocha in a deep sadness. His eyes were full of tears and his voice was shaky. Pranchú asked him what had happened and Alyocha told him that his father, Fyodor, had just been cruelly murdered. To make matters worse, the man accused of the crime was his older brother Dmitri, who had been taken into custody and would soon go on trial.

It was a difficult night and the minutes didn't seem to pass. Feelings of self-destruction and insanity mingled with that eccentric reality. It was a tragedy that felt like a satire, and both were part of the same truth. Pranchú was able to identify a very peculiar aspect of the Russians in the moment, which would later be translated in the words of Alyocha, according to whom the greatest happiness one can experience is when they discover why they are unhappy. Maybe it was the cold that froze the Russians' minds, but to them, living meant suffering and crying. That certainly was a Russian truth!

Pranchú also understood then that it was time for him to leave the dorm and breathe some lighter air, especially because the cold made the atmosphere in that region much heavier. In his letter to Alyocha about his intention to leave, Pranchú left a message that would perhaps change the destiny of that chimerical work:

"My dear friend Alyocha, the secret of existence is not only living, but also knowing what to live for! Stop taking sadness into account and start counting your joy!"

Pranchú asked to move in with Fyodor, his college pal, until graduation day, but also kept in touch with Alyocha, who always told him news about the brothers *Karaofmyeggs*. Pranchú always ended up telling the details to Fyodor, who became

---

[66] In free translation: *kara* means punishment, *mázat* means to make something dirty, and *meus ovos* means my eggs. In Russian, the phrase means something like "he who provokes his own punishment by behaving badly."

quite invested in the stories. The two friends drank and philosophized about the issue according to the so-called existentialism and worldliness of the brothers *karameuovos*. At the center of their philosophical speculation, which was based on the brothers' controversy, was Fyodor's incredulity of other individuals. In his drunken state, Fyodor would always say:

"The more I like humanity as a whole, the less I appreciate people as individuals."

When Pranchú's exchange programme ended and he returned to his native land, he began to appreciate more deeply the details and facets of the region, almost as if he were in one of Pedro Américo's famous paintings[67]. Because of the experiences he lived abroad, Pranchú started paying less attention to his scholarly laurels and more attention to the greatest gift of life: his native land and its spiritual happiness which could be freely enjoyed.

One day, years after his return, Pranchú was at a bookshop when he suddenly saw a peculiar book whose title seemed very familiar: *The Brothers Karamazov*, by Fyodor Dostoyevski. The book had become very famous because of its explanation of existentialist theory. Pranchú bought himself a copy and brought it home, where he read it in one sitting.

Reading the book brought Pranchú back to Russia and all the feelings he had lived at that time, especially the Russian feeling about tragedies that feel like satire and share the same truth. Unconsciously, he had planted a fruitful idea which was now being used, albeit furtively, by someone Pranchú truly respected. His first reaction was resentment towards his friend's stealthy attitude. Then, however, he felt admiration for his friend because he had transformed a very desolate, dismal story into a work about theology, psychology, and especially, existentialism.

Fyodor could not be criticized for taking hold of the idea, mainly because he himself had warned everyone about how he had less appreciation for people as individuals. In other words, Fyodor had already alerted everyone about himself and how he was bound to do something debasing, like taking someone else's idea. It never actually came to light though, and Dostoevski made his name as one of the world's greatest thinkers.

---

[67] Pedro Américo, born in the state of Paraíba, was one of Brazil's most prominent painters.

Pranchú also rejoiced in all of this because he had been able to do something he always preached: convince someone of an idea he created. He was reminded of an ancient moral aphorism which stated that "any idiot can paint a picture, but only a genius can convince someone to buy it." The words tranquilized Pranchú and made him think of another aphorism, which now he vigorously stated out loud:

"No idea is useless or idiotic. The best way to have a good idea is to have many ideas, even useless and idiotic ones!"

Thus said Pranchú!

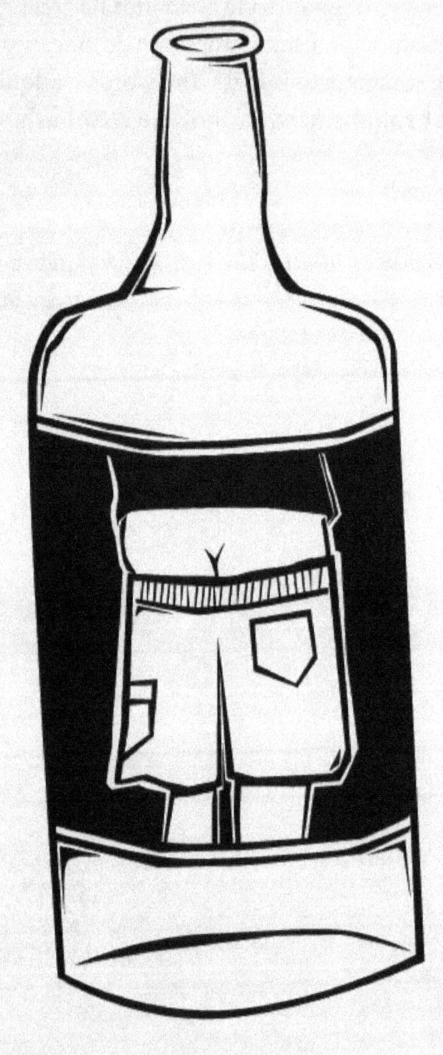

"BEBUM CULUS NON
PATRONUS EST!"

14

A PRAYER FOR THE YOUTH WHEN NO ONE ORA PRO NOBIS[68]

In some situations, embarrassment can be so masculine that it is more stirring than crucification. The penitent might even find himself with terribly bruised knees from atonement attempts, but occasionally the situation remains in the rotten memory of some bibliographies and cannot be erased. This was what marked the life of Rui Barbosa, a witness of secondhand embarrassment.

Rui Barbosa was a friend of Pranchú's when they were freshmen at the College of Law in Recife, curiously located on Asylum Avenue, around the year 1866. That's right, Barbosa had studied in Recife before going to São Paulo. Rui and Pranchú lived in the same dorm and, for this reason, began sharing books and secrets.

Despite being an undergraduate in his first year, Rui was so intelligent and skilled that he had already been offered an internship. It was at a fancy law firm in Recife and its most prestigious partner and shareholder was Rui's professor. In a short time, Rui was already doing the things most expert lawyers couldn't do, as if he had been practicing law for a long time. Due to all this virtue, the undergraduate was invited to participate in an important event at his prestigious professor's residence. It was an ostentatious luncheon whose guests had been chosen specifically due to their lineage and economic class within Recife's society.

Rui was thrilled with the situation, mainly because he had never had the conditions to be invited before. This was also reason for him to be feeling quite concerned with his part in the event, since he feared not adequately corresponding to the invitation he had received. Pranchú, who found this all to be quite funny, encouraged Rui and advised him not to take the situation too seriously, since it was merely lunch. Pranchú also told his friend that this would be an excellent

---

[68] *"Ora pro nobis"* is an Latin expression meaning "pray for us".

opportunity for him to do some networking and mingle with his peers.

"Rui, what if you find the future Mrs. Barbosa there?"

That was the last bit of encouragement Pranchú needed. So he went! When he arrived, very well-dressed in fact, he learned his first lesson of the day, one which could be referred back to a theory of microeconomics about an attorney making calculations (have you ever met an attorney who is good at calculations?). The lesson was that *"there is never any free food"*. This phrase became evident in the exact moment the undergraduate stepped foot in the mansion and was kindly conducted to its pompous office, where Dr. Varela de Assis Fagundes Varela, his professor and major partner at the aforementioned law firm, anxiously awaited.

Dr. Varela thanked the intern for his presence and informed him that there had been a sudden professional urgency which needed to be solved immediately. It was a habeas corpus, an inevitable constitutional remedy that needed to be filed in the judiciary duty the following day, a Sunday, and that the only one who could help was the young lawyer-to-be. An unusual situation, indeed. In the future, Rui would say that in that moment he remembered Pranchú's words: "It's what you get for being fucking awesome!" Ultimately, though, he had no choice.

The young man agreed to help, as long as there was a plate of chicken and sugar-free lemonade by his side, to help him focus. He got to work - *atrium, header, synthesis of the claim, facts*, and a long reflection on illegal coercion and abuse of power, legal requirements that resembled his current situation. During his break, which had a time limit overseen by the mansion's butler, he was offered a piece of cake and some water. Why serve anything else to someone working on a Saturday? After long hours of getting intimate with an elegant Remington, at about 9 pm, the heroic remedy was ready to be filed the next day.

Rui was exhausted and his only intention by then was to leave as soon as possible so as to avoid being asked to write up another *periculum in mora* or to do some more extra hours, without his workers' rights. Evidently, the intern wasn't, and couldn't possibly be, enthusiastic about the event anymore, unlike the other attorneys from Dr. Varela's practice and, of course, the other guests. By now, they were all more inebriated than the 0,2 g/l (0,02%) permitted by any blood alcohol test. Some of the guests were so beyond the state of inebriation that they had now reached a state of emotional turmoil. An evident psychiatric case.

As the undergraduate tried to leave without being noticed, he was approached by Madame Letícia Varela, Dr. Varela's wife at the time. Well-versed in the social graces, Mrs. Varela thanked Rui for helping her husband earlier and said that if it weren't for him, Dr. Varela wouldn't have been able to participate in the luncheon. She kindly offered Rui a drink, which he politely declined. In that instant, the master of the house appeared.

Like one who carries a trophy, Dr. Varela brought the intern to a round of drunkards who were talking about a whole bunch of nonsense. The jokes in bad taste disagreed with the sophistication of the mansion, but showcased the original pedigree of those sycophants. In fact, the hairier the joke, the louder the laughter grew.

Dr. Varela was now at the height of his drunkenness and need for attention. He called his wife over, dragging her by the arm, and asked all those present to be silent. He told them he had a story to tell about the two of them. Mrs. Varela had a desperate look on her face while everyone else encouraged the drunken husband to tell his tale:

"Tell us, tell us, tell us! the crowd sang."

As expectation filled the room, the crowd grew silent. Gripping his wife's arm, Dr. Varela began speaking in that honest and sacred tone that only a third stage of drunkenness can provide. He loudly said:

"You see this woman here? She is quite the firecracker in bed and does electrifying things, if you know what I mean…"

If that wasn't awkward enough, Dr. Varela made it worse with gestures involving his thumb, index, and middle fingers, which caused the most incredulous lookers-on to furrow their brows in awe. Who could imagine that Mrs. Varela, so pious, gracious, and demure, could take part in something lewd and unimaginable? To make the awkward situation even more intense, Dr. Varela added:

"And the worst part is that I enjoy it! Could that be considered homophilia?"

Red with embarrassment and distress, Mrs. Varela ran off at the fastest pace in history, probably a hundred meters under ten seconds, a record beaten only a century later by the American athlete Jim Hines. Rui took the chance to joke about how Mrs. Varela's disposition seemed to be at the speed of light. This, he thought, was a great pun related to electricity which directly referred to the words Dr. Varela had used and to his three-pronged finger gesture. The image of the latter, in fact, was now indefinitely burned into Rui's brain.

After an entire afternoon without a single sip of wine and with so many boring jokes, Rui actually thought the one he had just said out loud was actually pretty good! As he was about to open his mouth to smile, he noticed that the drunkards at the end of the room - the ones who knew exactly what to do with their own (rear) ends - had stopped laughing. In a sudden movement, the first one raised his voice and hand and said:

"Thank you, Varela! The event was wonderful, but now I must be going. Good night!" The others followed suit and were off.

Even though Rui was still thirsty for the wine he hadn't tasted, he couldn't find an alternative to also saying goodbye to the master of the house and starting back to his own humble abode.

On the following Monday, Dr. Varela did not show up at his firm. On Tuesday, he wasn't seen there either, nor did he go to the university. On Wednesday, he sent a work related note to his secretary and to another lawyer, but didn't actually step into his office. On Thursday, he also didn't go to the university and said it was because he felt *engolesmado*[69], but was seen at the firm for five minutes at the end of the day. On Friday, at about 4 p.m, Dr. Varela remembered he had to deal with the habeas corpus that had been ready since the fateful day of his "revelation". He hurriedly dealt with it, after wasting nearly a week's worth of time because of the embarrassment.

When he arrived home, Rui was unsettled by the situation. He said:

"Justice examines infraction, details guilt, and inflicts penalty. Police and political administration prevent, impede, and combat anarchy!"

"What happened, Rui?" asked Pranchú.

"That was the phrase I used in the atrium of the constitutional remedy I left

---

[69] *Engolesmado* is a regional term from the Brazilian state of *Rio Grande do Sul*, located in the south of the country, and it means to be sick of everything and everyone.

on that bastard's desk last Saturday. I can only imagine the situation of the person in prison who still hasn't had his rights for defense due to the simple fact that Dr. Varela is resentful of his choices and moral attributes."

"And what are you going to do about it, Rui?"

"Not what I'm going to do, Pranchú, but what I've already done! I've alerted Dr. Varela about his responsibilities and described what I think is the path towards virtue. I don't think we should equivocate when it comes to our responsibilities, even if that imposes more tribulation upon us and even if it is dangerous to expose ourselves. We cannot neglect another human's defense rights because of our own moral incontinence!"

"And what else happened?" asked Pranchú.

"I was fired from Dr. Varela's law firm and he suggested I transfer to another university."

"And what are you going to do now?"

"I won't equivocate! I asked to transfer to Largo de São Francisco."

And that was Pranchú and Rui's quick and undescribable time together. They kept in touch by sending each other letters, but never met again in person.

In 1920, when Rui was old and in poor health, he sent Pranchú a letter mentioning that he had been invited to be the commencement speaker that year for the graduating class of the University of Largo de São Francisco, in São Paulo. Rui decided to mail Pranchú the speech he had written for the occasion. In it, Rui talked about his journey as a student and a lawyer, he also gave the young graduates a lot of advice and made important considerations about the role of attorneys in our society. Rui said that his speech had been inspired by the time he had spent with Pranchú and by the reflections he had after the episode with Dr. Varela. At the end of the letter, Rui added a quote which would certainly be included in his speech:

"Do not quibble with your responsibilities, no matter how much trouble they impose on you and to how much danger they expose you."

And Pranchú, when answering Rui's letter, added a brief note to the text, suggesting that Rui take pride in what he had done during his time as a student in Recife, which had been an attempt of a *prayer for the* (imprisoned) youth in a moment when no one *prayed for us*. Pranchú told Rui that his speech was a brilliant lesson of faith and civility to young minds, like his own had been at that time. It was a precious message full of metaphors and in it the wisest teachings and most elevated advice could be found.

Still, as he congratulated Rui for his auspicious words, Pranchú reinforced that his friend should forget any old grudges linked to Dr. Varela. He mentioned that what happened between them had led to this inspiring speech, which Pranchú thought should be entitled *Oração aos Moços*[70], or a prayer for the youth. He added that it was too late to change the confessions of an old youth, which now echoed in the annals of the College of Law in Recife, and reiterated the old and wise adage declared by Pranchú himself:

"Bebum culus non patronus est!"[71]

Thus said Pranchu!

---

[70] *Oração aos Moços* is a famous speech by the great Brazilian writer Rui Barbosa. It was the commencement speech for the 1920 graduating class at the College of Law in Largo de São Francisco, in São Paulo. Due to his poor health at the time, Barbosa could not be there in person, but his speech was read by Professor Reinaldo Porchat. In it, there were reflections about the role of a magistrate and the mission of an attorney.
[71] *"Bebum culus non patronus est"* is a Latin expression which says that a drunkard's asshole belongs to none.

"IF YOU'VE STEPPED IN SHIT,
SPREAD OUT YOUR TOES!"

15

THE OPALESCENCE OF A BLUE AGATE

It was said to be a sacred place full of mysteries and several writers of the time wrote about its many legends. Silent Pool, this mystical place, is approximately 50 kilometers from London, the city where Pranchú was living in the year 1926. Silent Pool is a lake with calm waters and the opalescence of a blue agate, typical of springs that rise in landscapes of chalk bedrock, that is, those with little organic matter yet lots of flint and clean water. It was the perfect place to rest and enjoy a glass of good, locally produced gin called *Silent Pool Gin*, new to the market and made in a wood fired boiler and copper still. Despite the folkloric character of the place, what actually drew Pranchú in was the desire to see the production of this up-and-coming drink.

At the time, Pranchú was working as a taxi driver in London and had a very powerful Beardmore Mark III Hyper, a brand new model in those days, equipped with a 12.8 horsepower engine and with a reputation for being fast and maneuverable. After a lot of planning and saving up money, he would, at the end of his shift on the night of December 3, 1926, finally go on his long awaited trip to Silent Pool.

It was an easy and hassle-free journey. Near the entrance, Pranchú signaled a turn to the right, where he could access Silent Pool. Immediately after turning, though, Pranchú noticed an unusual situation. Too unusual in fact. A woman with a small suitcase was crying profusely and begging for a ride. She was wearing an overcoat and a Cloche hat, which was very common at the time, and had a fan with which she kept her face hidden. Even though Pranchu was no longer on duty with his taxi, there was no way to ignore the situation, after all, it was quite cold and already past 10:30 p.m. Pranchú got out of the car, opened the door and accommodated the passenger in the back seat. Then he spoke to her:

"Good evening, madam! I'm not on duty right now, but I can still help you. I'm staying here in Silent Pool, but I can drop you off at Guildford first, if you'd like. How are you?"

He wasn't sure if he should call her miss or missus. The woman answered:

"I would like you to take me to Harrogate!"

Pranchú was struck by the proposal - Harrogate was more than 400 km from Silent Pool. He suddenly thought that this order seemed rather arrogant. Before he could retort, the woman added:

"I'll pay you whatever you want."

Pranchú then became suspicious for several reasons. How, in the misogynist society of that time, could a woman be wandering alone at night? How could she afford such costs?" Then he said:

"It's not about money, madam. I've been planning a trip to Silent Pool for months. I'll take you to Guildford and from there you can find another ride. Alright?"

"Alright," she agreed.

When they were nearly halfway there, the woman suddenly cried resignedly and began to speak quite spontaneously.

"What makes a person cheat on another? I've helped him so much! I gave myself completely to him. What have I done?"

The woman was now sobbing as she brought up her marital situation. There was a moment of silence and then Pranchú said:

"Madam, if I may! While it can be comforting to create excuses to justify the behavior of those we love, we also need to recognize that each person is responsible for their own actions. No one should take the blame for the behavior or decisions of others."

"But there was betrayal and he has asked for a divorce. What have I done?"

"You did nothing. Sometimes these things happen and there's nothing we can do. And betrayal, well, everyone goes through it at one time or another."

There was a pause for reflection and, after some more tissues, the woman stopped crying. She then asked Pranchú:

"You're right. What's your name?"

"My name is Pranchú."

"Mr. Pranchú, how much would a taxi fare cost from Guildford to Harrogate?"

"I have no idea, but I know it wouldn't be cheap!"

And so the woman began looking for something in her bag. Pranchú could already imagine what it was. Before reaching Guildford, she asked him once again:

"Mr. Pranchú, how much would you charge to take me to Harrogate?"

"Madame, what's your name?"

"My name is Neele, Theresa Neele."

"You see, Ms. Neele, it's not about the money. As I mentioned, I've been planning my trip to Silent Pool for months, and there's no amount that would make me change that and go elsewhere.

"I understand, Mr. Pranchú. I just wanted to know how much you would charge to take me there."

"I see."

And so, Pranchú thought about it and gave her an astronomical figure. The amount was so absurd that no one would ever pay. The idea was to stop Ms. Neele from insisting that he take her on the trip. After she heard his price, she exclaimed:

"Wow! It's actually a considerable price!"

Pranchú continued trying to discourage her:

"I'm sure another driver would charge you far less for the same trip."

With disconcerting wit, the woman replied with the following consideration:

"You know, Mr. Pranchú, there is a big difference between price and value. I realize that the price for drivers in the city of Guildford may be less than yours, since you've added value to yours. Price is what you pay but value is what you get. I know you don't want to take me to Harrogate - at any cost - because staying in Silent Pool is valuable to you. That is very dignified because nowadays, although people know the price of everything, they don't value anything. You're either worth what you charge or you charge what you're worth. I admire your posture!"

Following this intervention, Ms. Neele removed a stack of money and placed it in the seat next to Pranchú. It was so much money that he was forced to stop the car on the side of the road. Before saying anything, Ms. Neele clarified:

"I'm not paying for your price, Mr. Pranchú, but for your value in having to take me to Harrogate. I'm sure this trip will be of great value to you and to me as well, believe me! You mustn't refuse."

Pranchú pondered everything internally. It was that eternal dialectic dispute between good and evil that exists in all of us. One side wanted to drop that lady off at the first corner and head straight to Silent Pool. The other side revisited periods of financial hardship and reminded him that: "the most sensitive spot in the human body is the pocket." The amount he would receive from the trip could probably guarantee his stay in Silent Pool another time, maybe more than once. What complicated dialectics!

Pranchú also considered the issue of value, as this fare and its conditions seemed to be a mission entrusted to him. Maybe the trip could be a good experience! If there was one thing Pranchú was aware of was that life was too short, as was his money. After much thought and consideration, he proclaimed:

"Alright, I accept. Not just for the money, but for the value that perhaps exists in this trip. Anyway, it will be tiring and we'll only arrive there in the morning."

"I am not in a rush, Mr. Pranchú. It will be an interesting journey."

Pranchú, ever cautious, carried two gallons of gasoline in his car, which would guarantee their trip throughout the night. And so, around midnight, they set out for Harrogate. Ms. Neele tried to sleep, as if to calm her past anguish. She turned from one side of the backseat to the other, but couldn't sleep. Pranchú, concentrated on the road, was quite calm and serene on the journey. It was a cold night and silence took over. What prevailed was the sound of the noise of the mighty Beardmore Mark III Hyper, but its hum was suddenly broken by the sound of a question from Ms. Neele.

"Mr. Pranchú, if I may - what do you do in your free time?"

"Ms. Neele, I work long hours during the day. In my free time, I can only think of getting some rest, drinking and reading the newspaper - but not necessarily in that order. Drinking and reading the news relaxes me."

"And what about reading the news relaxes you?"

"Well, when I have free time I open up a bottle of good scotch and read the police reports in the newspaper. It's as if they have lives of their own. You know, if I wrung that paper I'm sure I'd get drops of blood."

"Yikes, Mr. Pranchú. And you think that's good?"

"Sure! It's when reality meets fiction. In the newspaper, crimes are solved little by little and that makes a reader like me excited for the next day's publication. Sometimes there's nothing new about yesterday's crime on the paper, but then there's something about last week's crimes, and so on. It's as if the journalists know how to keep us entertained with all this police literature."

"Have you ever read a book about this?"

"Crime stories?"

"Yes, novels that tell stories about crime ans mysteries, that have plot twists or surprises…"

"Ms. Neele, I've always been a fan of Detective Dupin, by Edgar Allan Poe. And of course, our good old Sherlock Holmes by Mr. Doyle."

"Oh yes, Mr. Pranchú. Edgar Allan Poe was the author of many unslept nights in my childhood. And Sherlock Holmes has always inspired generations."

"Me too, Mr. Neele. When I was young I read *The Murders in the Rue Morgue*, *The Mystery of Marie Rogêt*, and *The Purloined Letter*, all by Poe. Those stories entertained me but also left me really intrigued. Even in Detective Dupin's stories, all the crime narratives had origins in newspaper reports. In *The Murders in the Rue Morgue*, for example, Detective Dupin first knows about the murders through the paper *Le Monde*. With Sherlock Holmes, it was no different, but I've only read a few of his stories, *A Study in Scarlet*, *The Sign of Four*, *The Hound of Baskervilles*, and *The*

Valley of Fear. In each of these stories there was some interaction with news reports, even to hire old Sherlock himself. It made me more curious about the newspaper than the novel. That's why I stopped reading those books and concentrated on the crime reports themselves."

"But to solve these reported crimes, Mr. Pranchú, there needs to be someone to investigate and provide solutions to society. That's why we have Detective Dupin and Sherlock Holmes."

"I agree, Ms. Neele, but the problem is that this type of hero only exists in fiction. In the newspaper, the police take over the investigation and the crimes are generally solved due to several variables."

"Sure, but there are real detectives who were important in the solution of those crimes. Have you ever heard of Eugène-François Vidocq? He was a private eye that became so successful in solving crimes he founded the National Police in France, which specialized in criminal investigations. He even became an inspiration for Victor Hugo and Honoré de Balzac."

"It's curious to me how a woman like yourself knows of such things!"

"Curious things, habits. Those who have them sometimes don't even know they do. Anyway, Mr. Pranchú, what's the problem? I'm just as curious as you, sir. And I like mystery stories."

"I can tell, Ms. Neele. After all, I did find you alone, on a cold night, in a strange place. It's very typical of a news report."

"Mr. Pranchú, I've just learned of my husband's adultery and that he wants a divorce. How will I do that? What will people think of me? Can you even fathom what I'm going through?"

"I can only imagine that it's a very complicated situation, Ms. Neele. I apologize!"

"Indeed. So I decided to leave the house and give him a scare. But I don't want to talk about him. Let's go back to the conversation about newspaper crimes and mysteries. What don't you like about crime stories with lead detectives?"

"I've got nothing against the detectives. I just think there's a lack of empathy between the detective and the readers. Take a look at Detective Dupin, he was very astute when solving mysteries, but too naive not to charge for his services. The stories were very good, but too surreal when contrasted with reality. Sherlock Holmes, on the other hand, was such an eccentric man that no one could identify with him. You see, he was as clean as a cat and at the same time as messy as a pig. He had a cunning that bordered on arrogance, as his faithful squire Watson described so well in *The Hound of the Baskervilles*. How to empathize with these two? You can't. I prefer the anonymity of newspaper heroes."

"I see. And how would you describe your ideal detective?"

"Oh, I wouldn't know for sure. Maybe an extravagant guy that's also kind of ordinary. Extravagant and short. I think people like characters like that because they see themselves in them, because they're noticeable wherever they go. A fellow who's not modest because of his intelligence, like Sherlock, and who's always elegant in appearance, typical of an original Londoner. Of course, nationality could be another way to camouflage the detective's pedigree."

"And what would you name this detective?"

"Being short, extravagant and intelligent, maybe I'd give him a name and last name that could contradict all of that, something strong and at the same time funny. Maybe the protagonist's name could already make the reader curious. But why did you ask me that? I'm not a fan of detectives!"

"I'm only curious, because it's incredible to me how someone could like police tales so much, with crime and mystery, and yet not be a fan of the protagonist."

"Not a fan at all. I enjoy the narrative of the real stories much more."

"Alright, Mr. Pranchú, and how would a true crime story get your attention?"

"Well, there's always the story about public enemy number one. Do you know it?"

"No!"

"In some news reports about crime, there's occasionally a famous criminal or fugitive dead in mysterious circumstances. People are surprised but relieved by the elimination of this public enemy in society. No one is dismayed and the investigations, generally, aren't taken any further. In this case, there are two great problems for the investigation: firstly, there's a great feeling of relief in the elimination of this public enemy and secondly, anyone could have been a suspect in the crime according to the dead criminal's police record. This creates such a difficult setting for scrutiny that it's easier to justify it in any way and give up on the investigation. To make matters even more complicated, maybe it would be intriguing if the crime occured in a scenario that included several countries, that is, something in motion like a train or an airplane, which would make it difficult to know which country's legislation the inspection should follow. Anyway, I think a real crime story that would draw my attention would be precisely one in which someone investigated the death of a public enemy."

"Wow, Mr. Pranchú, it would be a perfect storm for a crime. Magnificent! I think I'm having spasms of epiphany!"

"What do you mean, Ms. Neele?"

"Oh, nothing! I only mean that I became quite curious about the possibility of a novel with a similar story."

"I don't think there is one, because it's a crazy story I've just thought of and I highly doubt anything similar is out there. It's all a mixture of ideas that come from my daily news reports."

"I see. But still, it's a fantastic idea!"

And the conversation lasted the whole night of their journey until morning. The curious fact is that at no time did Ms. Neele remove her Cloche hat and always kept the fan close to her face, as if she didn't care to show herself. Pranchú did not mind that fact, but he did not fail to observe it. At around 11:00 am on December 4th, they finally arrived in the city of Harrogate.

"Ms. Neele, where would you like to stay?"

"Mr. Pranchú, I'd like you to bring me to the Swan Hydropathic Hotel."

"I'm not sure where that is, but I'll find it."

When they arrived, Pranchú was astounded by the beauty of the hotel. He realized that it was an environment of great luxury and refinement. At the entrance of the hotel, there was a huge billboard that said it was a spa with Turkish baths, an original hamam. Ms. Neele asked Pranchú to wait at the reception while she checked in, as she would like to thank him for taking her to Harrogate. When she returned, she accompanied Pranchú to the car and handed him another small stack of money.

"Ms. Neele, there's no need to pay me again. I've already been well paid!"

"Mr. Pranchú, as I've said, I'm not paying for the price of something, I'm repaying you for the value of your kindness in bringing me here despite your wish to stay in beautiful Silent Pool."

"Thank you, Ms. Neele, but I cannot accept this because it was not what we agreed on."

"Mr. Pranchú, this trip was much more valuable to me, believe it. The essence of life is to go forward, with no possibility of even trying to march backwards. In fact, life is like a one way street. I had a lot of fun on our journey and have certainly gotten something out of it. Keep this money and feel no remorse in doing so."

"But Ms. Neele…"

"No more of this, accept it in good faith! I only ask that you be discreet about everything that happened last night and, if possible, don't mention my whereabouts to anyone if someone were to ask. I want to give my husband a good scare."

"Alright. Regarding your situation with your husband, I'm not sure what you intend to do, but whatever you decide, go on, after all - if you've stepped in shit, spread out your toes!"

Pranchú thanked her once again and started on his way back to London, where he would arrive by nightfall. He was quite tired after being awake for thirty hours, so he slept in on that end-of-autumn Sunday morning. It was nearly noon when he woke up, and he decided to buy some ingredients to make a nice lunch accompanied by that very Silent Pool gin he longed for and the day's newspaper. It was December 5.

After a few shots of gin accompanied by Scottish eggs, fish and potatoes, he started doing what he enjoyed most: reading the police reports of the day. He had bought *The Times and Manchester Guardian*, as well as the *Daily Mail and The Daily Express* tabloids. He proceeded to devour them quickly, as he always did.

A piece common in all the newspapers caught his attention. It was the mysterious disappearance of an amateur writer named Agatha Christie, who lived in London, in the Styles region. The writer's car, a Morris Cowley, had been found with headlights on in a ravine on the lake at Silent Pool on the morning of December 4th. Inside the car were a pair of gloves and an elegant fur coat. The story was getting really interesting as there were so many people looking for her, including offers of £100 for anyone who had any information. There were divers in the lake at Silent Pool, scouts searching nearby regions, and thousands of volunteers looking for her. Even airplanes were made available. According to the newspapers, it was the first time that planes were used to search for a missing person in England.

Every newspaper carried the exact same photograph of the missing writer. In it, she sat in profile and was directly facing the photographer. Pranchú immediately noticed something very familiar and easy to recognize when he saw the photo. Despite attempts to hide herself with a Cloche hat and a fan, the missing writer was Ms. Neele.

Pranchú was astonished by the discovery. He immediately began to feel that he was part of a crime. How could I have been involved in a crime if it didn't happen? Pranchú kept thinking about the number of people who were looking for the writer and the deception that had been created around her disappearance. She was deceiving everyone, including Pranchú. At that moment, Pranchú decided he would go to the police and report on the whereabouts of the missing writer, who by now was reeling in the news in a Turkish bath at the spa in Harrogate. He changed his clothes, got in his car and went to the police.

He parked near the London Metropolitan Police and, while still in the car, thought about what had happened with Ms. Neele exactly one day ago and everything they had exchanged. The betrayal suffered by Ms. Neele, or in this case the writer Agatha Christie, seemed to be something very vivid. Plus, Pranchú had promised not to reveal her whereabouts to anyone, as she wanted to give her ex-husband a good scare.

Pranchú also remembered Ms. Neele's words: price is what you pay and value is what you get. And there was so much value in that crazy night he took Ms. Agatha Christie to her hiding place away from everyone. Pranchú realized he had taken part in the story of a very well-planned disappearance. She, Ms. Neele or Ms. Christie, knew very well that only Pranchú could drive her, which is why she was quite generous to him when paying for his service. There was no way Pranchú could hand her over to the police, however, he decided to keep an eye on all the mess.

In the days that followed, the tabloids began releasing new clues and information about the case. The police discovered that her husband, Archibald Christie, had a mistress and so he became the main suspect in his wife's disappearance. That was the information Pranchú wanted in order to confirm if Ms. Neele, or Agatha Christie, had told him the truth. According to the tabloids, the couple had been distant for some time and their relationship worsened after the writer developed depression when her mother had died. Mr. Archibald Christie told the tabloids he feared for his wife's life.

The information published in the papers agitated the British and there was no mention of anything else in the country. People began reading the newspapers as if they were reading a book written by the author herself. The biggest concern at that moment was the writer's daughter, Rosalind Christie, who was only seven years old. The British government wanted to solve the case as soon as possible to show off how efficient their police were. Even Sir Arthur Conan Doyle, the writer and creator of Sherlock Holmes, then 67, joined the search for Agatha Christie. A spiritist, Doyle took the gloves left in the writer's car to a medium in the hopes of a clue.

After ten long days, the tabloids reported that a musician had told the police he had seen Agatha Christie at a luxury hotel in Harrogate. The police decided to check the information, investigators went to the scene and discovered that Agatha Christie had checked in under the name Theresa Neele, the same last name as her husband's mistress. While she was there, she had enjoyed her stay in a very sociable way, and had even sung with the musician who would later reported her to the police. The writer presented herself to the police with confusion, as if she had had some kind of memory loss, and didn't even recognize photos of her daughter or her husband.

Despite the end of the incident, the tabloids continued to speculate. The writer's family stated that Agatha had lost her memory after the car accident and, because of that, decided to seek psychiatric help, without ever reaching a diagnosis. Others speculated that she had planned revenge against her cheating husband with the help of a partner she had never met before. There was also the idea that the disappearance could have been a strategy to increase the sales of her latest book, *The Murder of Roger Ackroyd*, released only weeks before the incident. The investigations into the case came to nothing, no one was indicted and everyone was satisfied with the simple reappearance of the writer.

Pranchú never again met Ms. Neele, now the famous writer Agatha Christie, but began reading all her work. In fact, Pranchú noticed that the character she created, Detective Hercule Poirot, resembled the one he had described on their trip on the night of December 3, 1926, despite the fact that the protagonist had already been created by the writer before that. Pranchú considered it a mere coincidence, although the description of the detective became more and more emphasized in the writer's later books.

A few years after the incident, in 1934, Agatha Christie released a book called *Murder on the Orient Express* with the exact plot Pranchú had shared with her on that trip from Silent Pool to Harrogate. It was the perfect storm, recalled Pranchú, and it became one of the writer's most famous books.

Speaking of Silent Pool, Pranchú finally visited its calm waters some years later. By then, the place had become quite folkloric as it was the place where the disappearance of Agatha Christie had started. Pranchú could finally taste Silent Pool Gin in its birthplace and enjoy the calm waters of the region. When swimming in one of the lakes, Pranchú found a blue agate and observed its opalescence. Suddenly, Pranchú had an epiphany - the opalescence of the blue agate was the essence of what Agatha Christie had experienced. It made sense to him when he remembered a phrase said by the then Ms. Neele as they were on their journey:

"The essence of life is to go forward, with no possibility of even trying to march backwards. In fact, life is like a one way street."

Perhaps she had been trying to tell Pranchú that she did not regret anything she had done so far and that, even if she did more, she would not regret it either. Life never stops, it doesn't forgive and it doesn't wait, it just goes on. And Pranchú, still in his thoughts, remembered how he motivated Agatha Christie to go on with her farce with an argument that was exactly the opposite of the opalescence of a blue agate. If you're going to do something you don't want to regret, go on and do it. After all:

"If you've stepped in shit, spread out your toes!"

Thus said Pranchú!

"TO STAY SANE, YOU MUST
ACT CRAZY SOMETIMES!"

16

PRESENTING SARTRE TO BEAUVOIR BY MEANS OF THE PRANCHURIAN EXISTENTIALIST METHOD

"One is never a man until he finds something he would be willing to die for."

A phrase that is strong for its meaning, but weak because of its lack of connection to the spirit, especially since it originated from an odd search for unrequited love.

Very well, Pranchú was working at a democratic bar on Rue Mouffetard at the Quartier Latin in Paris, in the year of 1928. The usual crowd at the bar were students from the University of Paris (Sorbonne), and they came from all over the world. The bar had quite an intriguing name: *Le Confessional* (The Confessional). In its entrance, there was a famous phrase that one day would mark many dissertations and theses: *Le confessional est notre bloc opératoire* (The confessional is our operation room). It was the right place to escape the traditional bistros and to reflect about life's pleasantries.

Pranchú, who worked there as a bartender, cook, waiter, and cashier, ran the place in the owner's absence. He was an outstanding worker and did not have much free time to digress about the political perspectives frequently discussed at the bar. He didn't lean right nor left, and surely didn't find himself in the center either. He had learned to stay out of discussions and presumptions, after all, survival was a priority for him. *Le Confessional* was known to be the last drink of the night and many intellectuals from Sorbonne were often there. Sometimes, dissidents from other institutions would also show up, like the ones from the very traditional French school *École Normale Supérieure*.

And it was from the *École Normale Supérieure* that came one of the bar's most frequent clients. A strange fellow, a bit spoiled, very polite, and always well-dressed - or as we say in the countryside, the perfect stereotype of a boy raised by his grandma. He was so self-centered that he didn't have any friends, but he liked going to the bar and spending hours talking to old Pranchú. He would spend all night with a single glass of wine and a cheese tray. Pranchú always said to him:

"I bet if you could, you'd even talk to yourself. You'd start a discussion, lose your reason, and then you'd be quiet."

The fellow would laugh and reply:

"I was born to satisfy the great need that I had for myself. I am an existentialist by nature, my noble friend."

He didn't have that typical and traditional Parisian arrogance because his was an arrogance focused on itself. The fellow's name was Jean-Paul (John Paul), or simply Jean to Pranchú, and the latter would usually tell the former off when the conversation circled back to him, which it usually did. Jean seemed to like it when Pranchú told him off, since apparently no one else did so.

Other clients were more nonchalant, they would make jokes and perform the traditional mise-en-scène of the time. They would sing politically enthralling songs or Italian operas to provoke the ladies around them.

"La donna è mobile, qual piUma al vento
Muta d'accento, e di pensiero."

This sequence would repeat itself and its conclusion normally involved the same odd figure: a prospective student at the University of Paris who was tough, determined, brave. She usually was the one to end their singing by use of heavy name-calling, spewing profanities such as scoundrels, fools, cons, rascals, and others. Her name was Simone and she was a feminist by birth with a refined taste for French liquor. Despite her Catholic upbringing, Simone completely escaped the stereotype of a French woman from that era. She even disapproved of the familial institution. A true whirlwind of a woman.

Le Confessional was always bustling and immersed in a lot of culture and antagonisms. It was an organized racket, and those who disorganized it must get their clothes and leave, as Pranchú would often say to his clients. Opposites co-existed harmoniously there: it was no place for quarrels.

One day, however, Simone nearly lost her mind with a friend of hers, René Maheu. He had invented a new nickname for her and she apparently did not like it.

"Beaver?"

"Calm down, Simone. It's 'Beaver' because of the animal's strong work ethic."

"Maheu, va te faire foutre!"

The discussion became so notorious that the nickname would later reach Sorbonne. Jean, the laconic, had been bothering Pranchú while he watched the scene. Dumbfounded, he asked:

"Pranchú, who is that woman? I've been observing her for quite some time here at Le Confessional. She's fascinating!"

"Jean, she's not your type. She's intelligent, cool, altruistic, tough, and has defined causes to defend. She's totally different from you. You, on the other hand, are no more than a grandma's boy. Be honest with yourself!"

Jean grew quiet for a moment and then reiterated the initial phrase:

"One is never a man until he finds something he would be willing to die for. I'm an existentialist, did you forget that?"

"That'd be profound if you hadn't forgotten the fact that it lacks spirit."

"What do you mean, Pranchú?"

"You can't wish for something you don't know how to get. What you lack, exactly, is the existentialism to react to the demands of life."

"Love, careers, revolutions. So many other things that start without knowing how they'll end. What to do, Pranchú?"

"Free yourself! Try to act in favor of the improvement of personal and human liberties, like she does. All experience is subjective and capable of being altered with willpower. Don't be fooled into believing that choices are restricted by circumstance and that, because of this, we can't be blamed for our actions. Exist according to your essence! The true journey is not measured by length, but by depth!"

And on that day Jean did something he had not yet done at *Le Confessional*. He got terribly drunk. He drank, vomited, embarrassed himself, tried to start a fight, and finally fell asleep. On that day, Jean finally, truly existed. After this episode, the youth didn't return to *Le Confessional* for a while, perhaps because he was ashamed or maybe there was another reason. Pranchú was only told that Jean had been studying a lot and was preparing himself for the feared entrance exam for a Master's degree at the University of Paris (Sorbonne).

One night, Jean showed up again. This time, though, he was feeling low-spirited and lacking his usual surreptitious motivation, like that of someone who always had something to hide. On that night he seemed really sad and went straight to the point:

"Pranchú, I failed the Master's entrance exam. Get a bottle of your cheapest Bordeaux and kindly pour me a glass, please!"

Upon examining him, Prachú saw his teary eyes and realized how miserable the youth was. He asked him an odd question for that moment:

"Hi there, friend, what the hell is this about? Are you really going to feel sorry for yourself? You are nothing like the fellow who was here last week!"

"My strange feelings from last week seem ridiculous today - I can't even access them anymore," Jean answered, unconvincingly.

"Jean, if life gives you lemons, make a *caipirinha* with it. If you don't drink caipirinha, then get some salt and tequila. If life is still too bitter because of that lemon, make sure you look everywhere carefully because you might find sugar when you're down in the dumps. Just don't let apathy take over you when you're facing adversities. Sometimes opportunity will knock on your door and you won't even notice."

In that instant, Simone and Maheu entered the bar holding each others' hands. Pranchú knew that Simone was Jean's platonic love interest, an unrequited romance because of the youth's own inertia or, in other words, because he lacked existentialism in his veins. Pranchú saw that Simone and Maheu were looking for a table in the crowded bar, so he had a brilliant idea.

"Jean, dry your tears, fake a smile, drink, and don't forget to move!"

"What do you mean, Pranchú?"

"Opportunities are constantly changing from place to place, and that favors those who are in movement. Moving is a part of existentialism, my friend. Follow my lead!"

Pranchú walked towards Simone and Maheu and invited them to sit at the table with Jean. They asked Pranchú if there would be any problem sitting at that table, and he replied that it would be his pleasure to introduce them to a young existentialist mind of that time, one who was applying to the Master's degree at the University of Paris (Sorbonne). The couple was intrigued and looking forward to meeting Pranchú's friend, so they sat down next to Jean.

The conversation lasted all night and, after various bottles of Bordeaux, Jean was back to being the fellow he was the week before. Before paying the tab, Simone called Pranchú over to thank him for the chance to sit with Jean. She mentioned how that night had been a delight. Pranchú, feeling that the moment was light and that there was a synergy between them, asked Simone for an unlikely favor.

"Well, since there was such empathy among you, why don't you two help Jean study for his entrance exam for the Master's at Sorbonne?"

Jean's face suddenly became red with embarrassment before René Maheu could answer.

"I was actually going to help Simone study for that exam. Jean, would you like to join our study group? The only problem is that the exam is not until next year."

Jean didn't even blink.

"Of course, I would love to!"

Simone sealed their deal:

"Then it is done! Let's start our study group. Sorbonne better get ready!"

The three of them began hanging out and were never seen apart. They often went to *Le Confessional* to study and hydrate their minds with a good Bordeaux. Pranchú noticed how Simone was getting closer to Jean, something René Maheu didn't see or didn't seem to be bothered by.

And low and behold! On his second attempt to pass the exam, Jean had the highest score. Simone had the second highest. They celebrated at *Le Confessional* with the best bottle of Bordeaux and in the presence of various study mates.

After starting his Master's degree, Jean went less often to *Le Confessional* because of the heavy study load. Rumors started going around the campus that Jean had stolen Simone from Maheu, and they had started an existentialist relationship that was far from monogamous. Other than their amorous relationship, there certainly was intellectual affinity between them, especially because they both had the pleasure of publicizing the creative processes behind their studies and publications.

Jean-Paul definitely grew wings, flew very high, and never appeared at *Le Confessional* again. From afar, however, his accomplishments were recognized. He had written novels, short stories, philosophical treatises, political essays, theatre plays. He had been imprisoned during the Second World War and taken part in several political parties. He became an intrepid and distant writer, which was not any news to Pranchú. He remained firmly beside his inspirational muse, Simone de Beauvoir, not worrying about how they were together. The fact was that they were together and they always helped each other's professional and personal growth, something hard to find at the time.

Thirty-two years after their last meeting, Jean-Paul returned to *Le Confessional* where he saw his priceless friend Pranchú, who now owned the place. Jean-Paul walked toward Pranchú and hugged him tightly.

"One is never a man until he finds something he would be willing to die for. I'm an existentialist, have you forgotten that?"

Pranchú replied:

"That would be profound if not for its lack of connection to the spirit"

It was their own special way to greet each other. Jean, now known worldwide as Sartre (a more arrogant name than "grandma's boy", as he was referred to before fame) told Pranchú about his wanderings and adventures up until the year 1960. He tried to explain his theory about existentialism and self-determination, where liberty would be the most important motif and would be reflected in the conditions of a being's existence. He said:

"Pranchú, we are doomed to be free."

"That's right, dear Jean. I'm happy about your adventures, but in your origins your freedom was stunted by your lack of existentialism. Thank Simone, she freed you from yourself."

"That's true, Pranchú. Doomed and free. Doomed because one doesn't create one's own self and, yet, free because once launched into the world, one is responsible for one's every action.

And to crown his friend's adventures, Pranchú declared, with moral vaseline, the existentialism attached to the wind and disseminated into the whole world:

"Jean-Paul - To say sane, you must act crazy sometimes"

Thus said Pranchú!

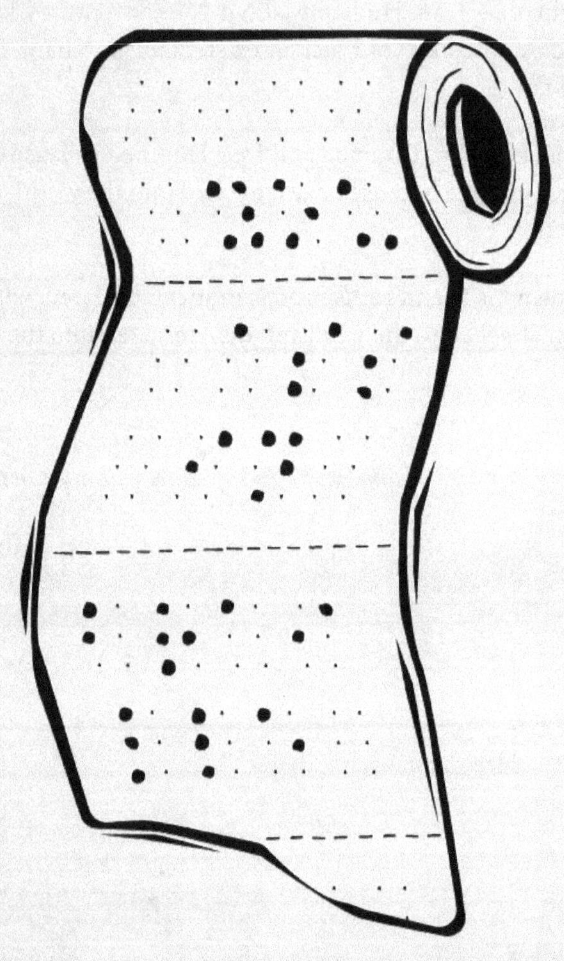

"WHY IS TOILET PAPER
PRINTED IN HIGH RELIEF
IF ASSES CAN'T READ
BRAILLE?"

17

DISCIPLINE AND PUNISH, PERHAPS REWARD!

The order was clear: to elaborate an innovative cultural project. Now, after signing the contract, all that was left to do was find a solution to this problem. As far as culture was concerned, Pranchú immediately remembered an individual he had met a few years back who had introduced himself as a "cultural ambassador" and who knew everything about the topic and its projects at the time. He would be perfectly suited to help on this mission.

Pranchú decided to look the fellow up and discovered, first, that he was working at a Parisian school named *Collège de France* and, second, that in addition to their lack of contact in while, he also wasn't very easy to locate. Mica, as Michel was kindly nicknamed by his longtime friend Pranchú, owed the latter a debt of gratitude, which was why he did not hesitate in saying yes when his friend asked for help.

"Mica, I urgently need your help!"

"Of course, dear Pranch! I'm all ears."

"I was hired by a media company to develop a truly revolutionary entertainment project unlike any other available nowadays."

"Do you have anything in mind?" asked Michel.

"I imagined a program that could be interactive with real life, like a game. A reality show that highlights situations and events which results from the reality of coexistence. I thought it would be interesting to watch strangers live together in real time."

"Wow, Pranch, what a phenomenal idea! How do you intend to do it?"

"That's just where you come in, my friend. I know that you are quite shrewd and avant-garde, and that's why you can certainly come up with the perfect format for this project."

"And how long would it last?"

"One week," answered Pranchú.

"I normally wouldn't have the time to help, but for you I'll make an exception! I'll narrow down some of my ideas and present you with a tentative project by next week."

A week later, after many unslept nights, Michel met with Pranchú to show him an outline of the theoretically revolutionary project.

"So, Michel, did you come up with something?"

"I did, my friend. It's a project based on the *"Panopticon"*!"

"Pan what?" asked Pranchú.

"*Panopticon*, my friend!"

"And what is that?"

"Last week, coincidently, I was reading some articles about disciplinary devices utilized in ancient European prisons. That's when I stumbled upon the *Panopticon*, an idea conceived by the English philosopher Jeremy Bentham. His idea was to create an observational structure within prisons, asylums, schools, hospitals, or factories. Evidently, the study ends up constructing a system of moral philosophy…"

Pranchú, interrupting the explanations, anxiously asked:

"Ok, but how can we use that in practical terms?"

"Well, the idea is to create a structure for the confinement of people that is incorporated into an observation tower in the center of a circular building, called a 'rotunda', which is divided into two rooms. Each of these rooms is large enough to have two windows: an exterior window, for light to enter the room, and an interior window facing the observation tower. Walls would isolate the occupants of each room, who in turn would find themselves subject to collective and individual scrutiny by a watchman in the tower who would remain hidden from them. I think blinds or shutters could cover the windows of the observation tower, and there should be maze-like connections between the rooms and the tower in order to avoid flashes of light or any noise that could reveal the presence of the observer. At certain times of the day, the participants could be together in a common environment. The general idea is to observe the subjects in their solitary moments as well as moments when they coexist with others."

"Well, the idea of observation and vigilance is quite good, but how would it work as a game?" asked Pranchú.

"We could create various rules of coexistence for those who participate, such as the rule of minimum quantity, the rule of sufficient ideality, the rule of collateral effects, the rule of perfect certainty, the rule of common truth and the rule of ideal specification."

"Please, Mica, don't overdo it with your philosophy! The idea of rules of coexistence is good, but maybe we can make them a little simpler."

"But, Pranch, the idea of coexistence is already simple. For example, the rule of sufficient ideality presupposes the idea of torment. That means those who don't comply with the tests determined by the director of the program will be penalized."

"How illogical!" shouted Pranchú.

"Not at all, if the idea is to observe and punish those who don't comply. The last one there wins the game! Another example is the rule of ideal specification, which presupposes that the program has a code of conduct that must be followed by all participants. Those who don't follow it will be punished."

"Mica, that is as philosophical as it is illogical. So much so, though, that it might work!" replied Pranchú.

"Creating this type of disciplinary program might be very educational for the families who watch. The idea is to discipline and punish them. Those who receive the least amount of punishments take the prize."

"Mica, despite my reservations, I am actually convinced that this is a good project. Now I have to convince the producers and the people who will finance the program. They're new investors in the entertainment business and they don't seem to know much about this market. I'm going to name this outline *Project Charter*, establish its premises, requirements, investments, schedule, etc. Bottom line - I will try my hardest to sell this project."

"Luck be with you, Pranch!"

Two weeks later, Pranchú presented his project to *John de Mol and Joop van den Ende*, partners and businessmen who had recently entered the Dutch entertainment industry. At first, they thought the project was meant to be some type of comedy program, since recording people living together on a daily basis would surely result in amusing situations, especially considering the human psyche. There was no denying the fact that the daily documentation of someone grumbling, flatulating, snoring, and making other bodily sounds would be really hilarious.

Still, the project contemplated other situations that could be appreciated socially, such as observing the coexistence of different kinds of people as a way to reflect on society itself. It was all too beautiful and philosophical for entertainment purposes, explained Mr. John de Mol, and perhaps a bit too advanced for the time, he clarified.

"My dear, Pranchú, I was truly impressed with this project. It's much more than I imagined."

Mr. John de Mol, who was full of ideas inspired by a certain fellow named Guy Debord, opened a page in a book entitled *The Society of the Spectacle* and read a small excerpt out loud:

"The spectacle is ideology par excellence, because it exposes and manifests in its fullness the essence of all ideological systems: the impoverishment, servitude and negation of real life. The spectacle is materially 'the expression of the separation and estrangement between man and man.'"

Pranchú, who didn't understand a word of it , asked:

"What about the project?"

"You see, Pranchú, I was so impressed with the project that I cannot endorse it. You're right, observing different people living together can be a reflection of society, but perhaps society is not yet ready to meet itself, at least not now. I'm going to postpone this project. That's my decision. I want to thank you…"

"But Mr. Mol," interrupts Pranchú. "The project can be implemented in practical terms! I can show you."

"Dear Pranchú, it's not the right moment. Society is not ready for this innovation. Now, how much do I owe you?"

"Nothing, Mr. Mol. Let's leave it for the future!"

Pranchú was very upset with the whole situation. He had built up a lot of expectation for the development of a project that would now only remain on a piece of paper. What's more is that he had made Michel waste a lot of time to create it. What if it affected their friendship? One thing is to lose a project, but it would be even worse to hold a friend back and waste their time.

Some hours after the disappointing meeting with the investor, Pranchú met up with Michel and stalled a bit before revealing the investors' verdict. Eventually though, Pranchú awkwardly started:

"Ah, friend, the news isn't good. Our project has been rejected. Actually, it's been archived because they weren't interested in launching it now…"

"That's great news, Pranchú!" interrupted Michel.

"Great news?" asked Pranchú.

"Of course, Pranch! I have finally found a thread for my studies! This project sparked in me an interest for a new theoretical movement called social anthropology. The observation of people by means of a game is a manifestation of habits, routines, customs, cultural evolution, among other anthropological manifestations. That's a great discovery, don't you think so?"

"Sure, I think so too! I was afraid you would be upset with the rejection of our project."

"Pranchú, if our project had been approved, I probably wouldn't have the chance now to develop work that could promote social politics. We would have to give up all personal rights over these ideas. I'm glad that those jackasses rejected the project. And as for me, well I intend to write something about discipline and punishment! What do you think?"

"Well, my friend, we did start this project together, but now this journey is all yours. I don't mean 'journey' only in a figurative sense, but also in a physiological and philosophical one. If you travelled this much only to contextualize a simple variety program, I can only imagine the transcendence you will go on to arrive at your final destination of *Discipline and Punish*. Remember, the ironies of destiny can sometimes be a great piece of shit, but they can also be surprising!"

The two smiled in relief, for different reasons. Pranchú was happy about the pleasant ending to this project and Michel about the promising start of a new one. The fact, though, is that destiny sometimes puts opportunities right in front of our eyes, but we insist on not looking. Some look and only observe, letting time do the work for them. Others try to hold on, however carelessly. And others are placated by opportunity itself.

Michel, after letting go of the numbing caused by structuralism and social anthropology, finally made his last name, Foucault, famous and synonymous with modern critical thinking, especially regarding social control.

The best part of it, who knew, had emerged from a crazy idea thought up by Pranchú in their proposal for an entertainment program which would give way to the creation of the book *Discipline and Punish by Michel Foucault*, years after its rejection by two newcomers to the television industry. Actually, it should be noted that the two producers who had rejected the project had quite interesting endings as well. *John de Mol* and *Joop van den Ende*, who had begun a long journey in the industry of Dutch entertainment, came together in a lasting marriage whose last name was also made famous: Endemol.

Endemol, a name formed by joining its partners' last names, became a well-known Dutch television production company, with great notoriety and expertise in, you guessed it, reality shows. The company develops formats and standards for television programs, based on reality shows, and sells them around the world to various television studios.

Despite the fact that Pranchú and Michel's project had been rejected long before the boom of reality television, it is not possible to disassociate reality programs from the old Panoptic, thought of by the English philosopher Jeremy Bentham and cited by Foucault in their outline of the project. These tv shows are probably more similar to the social theory in *Discipline and Punish* than our futile philosophy can ever imagine. Who came first though? It doesn't matter. What really matters is that the idea, which came from an odd fellow named Pranchú, is the basis for substantiating totally diverse conceptions. And that is exactly the point: identifying it. Identifying an opportunity means questioning the reason for its own existence, as Pranchú, the philosopher, would often say when facing the most introspective usual circumstances:

Why is toilet paper printed in high relief if asses can't read Braille?

Thus said Pranchú!

"THE SECRET OF LIFE
IS BOTH BEAUTY AND
PATIENCE. IF IT WORKS
OUT, BEAUTIFUL!
IF IT DOESN'T, PATIENCE!"

18

THE FLOWERS OF EVIL
AND THE SAME OLD SHIT!

"My friend, this is so childish that it's sublime! I'd even say that though it's primitive and haunting, it's actually stunning. How did you learn to do this?"

"I learned by reading and observing illustrations from an anatomy book."

"Really? Well, there we have it. That's why it's still a little dismal. Do you have any other drawings?"

"Sure I do. Here they are…"

After taking a good look at the drawings, Pranchú said out loud:

"Oh. It's all the same old shit!"

This was the conversation between Pranchú and young Jean, who were high school classmates for a short period in the 1970s, more specifically in 1976, when Pranchú was an exchange student in the United States.

They were both fans of Dr. Henry Gray and Dr. Henry Vandyke Carter, the authors of a famous anatomy book from the distant year of 1858, Jean was such a fan that he would always sketch anatomical caricatures in his notebooks. He said that he had learned to like anatomy because of an accident when he was still a kid, when his mother had given him a book on the subject. From then on, he became interested in learning more about it.

Those who didn't know him might think he could certainly become a good doctor, maybe even a good orthopedist, but that was far from true. Pranchú had met him in high school, when they were studying at the City-As-School, a public institution in West Village in Manhattan, New York. They spent a short period together, just enough time for them to share profound experiences in their awakenings of youth.

Looking at young Jean's drawings at the time, Pranchú thought those poorly diagrammed figures resembled ancient poetry, typical of a bohemian, wandering poet, as if he were prophesying the description of Jean himself in the near future. Actually, though, Pranchú was thinking about the famous French poet Charles Baudelaire.

Pranchú imagined that, like Baudelaire, Jean's drawings were inspired by real perceptions of what he had lived, as if he wanted to express himself through the creatures based on that anatomy book. For Pranchú, the illustrations had the same tone of symbolism as Baudelaire's work. It is well known that Baudelaire introduced what would one day be called *"symbolist poetry"*, full of mysticism, alliteration, onomatopoeia and themes linked to human death and spirituality which were heavily caricatured in those drawings by young Jean.

Pranchú asked Jean:

"Have you ever heard of Baudelaire?"

And he answered:

"Baude who?"

Then, Pranchú explained who Charles Baudelaire was and what he represented to the culture of the world. Also known as the *Crooked Angel*, according to Pranchú, Baudelaire's poetry was individualist in character, clearly opposed rationalism and scientism, and expressed fantasies, mysteries, mysticisms and the importance of the human unconsciousness. Baudelaire's verses broke barriers imposed by rationality with the creation of an oneiric and transcendental universe. While Pranchú explained all of this, Jean intervened:

"Hold on, Pranchú. I've never heard of this Baudelaire. Are you sure you're not describing me? Or are you making a joke?"

"No, no! I'm describing Baudelaire himself! Your drawings are more similar to his poetry than you think. Your drawings focus on intuition and totally disregard rationality and logic. You're as mad as Baudelaire. What if you are his reincarnation?"

"I don't know about that, but '*I am passionate about mystery, because I always hope to uncover it.*'"

With his brow furrowed, typical of almost certain uncertainties, Pranchú widened his eyes and said:

"Jean, you've just said one of Charles Baudelaire's famous phrases! Do you know him? Are you mocking me?"

"Pranchú, look at me and tell me with all honesty - do you think I should look this guy up?"

"Why not?" asked Pranchú.

"I'm not too crazy about technical literature, full of embellishments. To me, the more abbreviations the better! Life is already too tense to be too wordy. I don't know this guy and I don't have the slightest vocation to be a poet. At most, I could draw some poorly diagrammed figures somewhere, but that's it!"

Amazed by the synergy of the moment, especially because it added to the crazy idea that young Jean could be the reincarnation of Baudelaire, Pranchú had another equally insane idea. He asked Jean to make a new drawing in his notebook and bring it to school the next day, and Pranchú would make a brief statement. Well, the next day, young Jean brought the drawing and presented it to Pranchú.

"There it is, Pranchú! Is that really all you wanted?"

Pranchú, in his unique, low-key sincerity, immediately replied:

"Huh! It's all the same shit!"

Then, in an attempt to describe the indescribable, Pranchú started talking about the illustration which, in essence, looked like a cranium or a colored skull.

"Your drawing seems simple, but it is loaded with connotations. It's a sketch of a skull made from patchwork, with various parts that clearly don't match, almost as if they were randomly assembled, and it has a sneering grin. The undecipherable representations on it make the skull look like it has a large seam with drawings that could refer to some culture from another country or perhaps to a lost feeling. There are some code-shaped letters up here, as well as some indecipherable scribbles, maybe to create an air of mystery. I think it is a clearly dysphoric (as opposed to euphoric) drawing and it is quite disturbing. So, what do you think of my description?"

"Pranchú, other than 'the same old shit' comment, I agree with everything you've said. In fact, your description was much more exciting to me than my own drawing. What now?"

"Well, now I'm going to quote a little poem by Charles Baudelaire, something that immediately refers to your drawing. I've added a bit to its content. I just ask that you look at your artwork as you listen to the poem."

Pranchú opened his backpack and pulled out the book *The Flowers of Evil*, Baudelaire's main work, and started leafing through it as if he already knew exactly what to find and where it was. No sooner had he found it than he began to recite the poem. It was called "*The Love and the Skull*"[72]:

(Old Tail-piece)
With bold and insolent grimace,
Love laughingly bestrides
The bare skull of the Human Race,
And, as enthroned he rides,
Blows bubbles from his rosy cheek
Which soar into the sky

---

[72] **BAUDELAIRE**, Charles. *As flores do mal*. Tradução de Júlio Castañon Guimarães, 1ª ed. São Paulo: Penguin Classics Companhia das Letras, 2019, p. 385.
"L'amour et le crâne"
L'Amour est assis sur le crâne
De l'Humanité,
Et sur ce trône le profane,
Au rire effronté,
Souffle gaiement des bulles rondes
Qui montent dans l'air,
Comme pour rejoindre les mondes
Au fond de l'éther.
Le globe lumineux et frêle
Prend un grand essor,
Crève et crache son âme grêle
Comme un songe d'or.
J'entends le crâne à chaque bulle
Prier et gémir :
- " Ce jeu féroce et ridicule,
Quand doit-il finir ?
Car ce que ta bouche cruelle
Eparpille en l'air,
Monstre assassin, c'est ma cervelle,
Mon sang et ma chair!

As if, beyond the blue, to seek
The other worlds on high.
They ride with wondrous verve at first,
Reflect the sunny beams,
Then spit their flimsy souls, to burst
And fade like golden dreams.
I hear the skull at each renewal
Expostulate aghast —
"This game, ridiculous and cruel —
When will it end at last?
For what your cruel mouthpiece drains
And scatters, sud by sud,
Monstrous Assassin! is my brains,
My substance, and my blood.[73]

When Pranchú had finished reading the poem, Jean seemed inflamed and immediately said:

"Wow, Pranchú, what a sensational description! It was as if my drawing were in motion, as if the skull I created put forward dubious and ironic feelings, just like this poem does. It's like suggestive magic that presents itself through the senses as a concrete reality. How insane! Now I'm excited to create even more crazy things."

"Well, your drawings might mean something, you just haven't discovered what it is yet. The fact, though, is that your art was born with the signature of a poet from the past and perhaps it represents a future for you. Who knows? Maybe you can be successful repeating these poorly diagrammed drawings somewhere!"

"That's true, each stroke means something, as if it were inside each poem. This opens infinite paths to follow, with no doubts about who created the drawings. What holds us back is not who we are, but who we think we can't be. Thank you, friend Pranchú, for introducing me to Baudelaire."

Well, after a year of studying together, Pranchú and young Jean went on different paths. While Pranchú returned home at the end of his exchange program,

---

[73] Roy Campbell, *Poems of Baudelaire* (New York: Pantheon Books, 1952). Disponível em: <https://fleursdumal.org/poem/188>

young Jean, in 1977, wanted to use his art as a way to find his place in the sun alongside other established artists. That same year, young Jean and his colleague Al Diaz, who was also a contemporary of Pranchú at the City-As-School, started making graffiti in several abandoned buildings in Manhattan and, in the following year, both of them dropped out of school.

In 1981, Pranchú visited the city and, out of curiosity, decided to go see a very controversial exhibit, previously aware of what he would find there. The first piece he came across had a name that seemed familiar to him: *the skull*. It was similar, if not identical, to a drawing scribbled on a certain notebook he had seen a few years back. There was no doubt that young Jean had now become a great artist, recognized worldwide as Jean-Michel Basquiat. When contemplating the piece, Pranchú could not resist repeating out loud the remark he had made in the past:

"Huh. It's all the same old shit!"

No sooner had he uttered the words than Pranchú was surprised by a clearly familiar voice:

"Aside from the fact that you said it's the same old shit, I agree with everything."

It was young Jean in flesh and blood and dreadlocks. The two embraced effusively, as if they had a lot to talk about. After the typical questions and answers of those who haven't been in touch for a long time, Pranchú asked:

"My young Jean, is this 'SAMO Shit' thing really what I think it is?"

"Yes, my friend Pranchú! It's an abbreviation for 'Same old shit', a term Al Diaz and I came up with for our school paper. Since the idea was a bit crazy, we decided not to use it in the newspaper, but instead used it on some graffiti art we did throughout the city. SAMO, in fact, was the character who signed the graffiti and we wanted it to be like a religious entity. It didn't amount to much, as you may already know, because some projects and my friendship with Al Diaz were lost on the way. That's actually why "SAMO is dead" was created. Anyway, what matters is that the symbolism was so great in this piece that it became famous around the world. It wasn't what I wanted to happen, but it did."

"Well, you take a shot towards what you see and hit what you don't see. The piece was fantastic and it made you stand out. Where did you get the idea for it?"

"There was this guy from high school who used to say my drawings at the time were always the same old shit. Do you remember, my friend?"

"Yeah, yeah, yeah. And it's still the same old shit! In any case, as you said yourself, your work carries symbolism bigger than 'SAMO is dead', which means your art is no longer dead shit. It's now a living reality which still breaks with rationalism and scientism like it did in the old days, and it's still very similar to that classic poet from our days at school…"

"Charles Baudelaire, Pranchú! I'm grateful you introduced me to him. It was reading Baudelaire that I began to understand my own work and its subterranean, unconscious and obscure side that causes unnoticed discomfort in people and, at the same time, is explicit in its own simplicity. And because it is somber and explicit, my graffiti art gains a dimension of strength that highlights the relations of power and oppression that hurt so many people. All in all, it's something that people have assimilated slowly."

"How interesting, Jean! Sometimes we don't realize how much we can inspire people to discover their own light."

"I had no clue. When I realized it, I started illustrating and painting in a more natural way, even though it was blurred art which often made me ponder the evil in humans. This dynamic reminds me of a phrase from our poet Baudelaire: *'Evil is done without effort, naturally, it is a work of destiny. Good is a product of art.'* Good and evil are in my work, so the result of my art is a work of fate. Can this be the secret of life, Pranchú?

And with a tone of farewell, Pranchú stated what could one day be moral fuel in the life of the great Basquiat:

"My young Jean, from Baudelaire to Basquiat and from Basquiat to Baudelaire, you are like a great vessel of paradoxes in this immense sea of life. Keep doing what you like most and don't forget a simple mantra that may serve as a life purpose:

> *"The secret of life is both beauty and patience. If it works out, beautiful!*
> *If it doesn't, patience!"*

Thus said Pranchú!

"ACCEPT THAT ON SOME DAYS YOU ARE THE PIGEON AND ON OTHER DAYS YOU ARE THE STATUE!"

19

OXE[74], IT'S OSHO!

"Pranchú?"

"*Oxe*, it's Osho!"

"It's been a long time, my friend! How nice to bump into you here in the middle of nowhere!"

And that's how it all started. Pranchú, wandering in the middle of nowhere, was found by Rajneesh Chandra Mohan Jain, also known as Osho - the philosopher, religious leader, and orator of Dharmic traditions (multiple meanings of Indian religions) whose true talent, however, was found in the dissolute art of tantrism and its counterparts. Pranchú had known Osho since he was still Rajneesh, a humble professor from the neophyte times in philosophy and the tantrism of old India. They met in the middle of a dirt road in the countryside of Oregon, United States. Osho was going to a ranch while Pranchú was heading towards the city of Portland, in the northeast of that state. Pranchú continued the dialogue:

"Yes, it's truly been a long time. What a coincidence meeting you right here, in the middle of nowhere. What are you doing here?"

"I was a bit ill back in Bombay and had to come here to the United States to get treatment for my back."

"Really? Your back? Well, with so many tantric tricks you did back in India, you were bound to have some back problems. Meditating in all those Kama Sutra positions was surely going to cause you congenital scoliosis one day."

---

[74] "Oxe" is an abbreviation of the Brazilian Portuguese word "oxente", which is a popular colloquialism from Northeastern Brazil. It is considered an interjection and is used to express surprise or shock.

"Oh, Pranchú, it was serious! I nearly had to get back surgery. Some friends of mine invited me to live here in Oregon so I could be near urgent care. They even pitched in and bought a ranch so I could settle down here. I'm better now. I've started a new phase in my life called *silent heart-to-heart communion.*"

"Heart-to-heart, dear Osho? You must be up to something. I bet it's tantrism in groups!"

"Come on, Pranchú! You know me better than that. My philosophy aims at deconstructing archaic dogmas and psychological traps that imprison and limit human beings. My goal is to achieve a freedom which predicates self-realization and dignity in one's life. A spiritual quest which pervades one's existential experience…

Interrupting Osho, Pranchú stated:

"The search for spiritual satisfaction through the mastery of one's own senses, or in other words, tantric shenanigans, right?"

"No, Pranchú, that perspective is limited. I have said and defended that sexual orgasms, for example, offer a glimpse into meditation because in it, time and the mind stop…"

And Pranchú once again interrupted:

"Well, there we have it. The reason you have scoliosis is because of tantric meditation based on the epistemology of Kama Sutra."

"Let me finish, my dearest Pranchú. Meditation must be achieved by silence and through the latter we can reach truth and love, guided by our individual consciousness, with no intermediaries such as priests, politicians, scholars, or any other speaker - not even me."

"Sure, now let me see if I've understood, dear Osho. A person has a little transcendental intercourse, feels lighter, then meditates until they've reached truth and love. That actually has an interesting logic to it. Would you believe me if I told you I applied the same philosophy last week with my most recent girlfriend? I'm even starting to think I in fact like her… Oh, honestly, Osho! You must be trying to get me off, in all senses."

"Pranchú, the idea is to transmit an optimistic message that points towards a future where humanity is able to leave the realm of unawareness and, consequently, destruction, fear, and disaffection. Each person would be their own Buddha, remembering that which the immediate consciousness has forgotten."

"What crazy shit, Osho! There's no way that people actually embark on this trip."

"And that's where you're wrong! I have many disciples who follow my ideas, including those who bought the ranch for me. They set up a commune near the ranch and created a small town in my honor called Rajnesshpuram, the city of Rajneesh (Osho's original name)."

"Oxe! Did they really, Osho? They must be out of their minds."

Osho goes on.

"I believe my mission is to help the people of this planet. Actually, come to think of it, the entire planet, with rare exceptions, is ill. But it is a self-imposed illness. Freedom, as I've mentioned before, is the foundation of self-realization and dignity. Silence, in turn, is the communion between a creature and its divine and pure essence, able to reconnect through meditation in which one can experiment one's true self."

"How interesting! The only thing I have to say is be careful. Be careful because groups that become sectarian, that follow or are devoted to something, usually adopt radical measures to defend their point of view. You'll soon find someone as deranged or even more insane than you in this cult you've created."

"I have not created a cult, Pranchú, only a philosophy for living and developing. As I always say, any animal can grow older, but developing is the human prerogative. And only a few claim that right."

"Right! Go tell that to your followers!"

"Life will not stop so you can choose which way to go. Sometimes, however, it's best to just 'listen' to your heart and be happy."

"True, Osho, from all the antics you've told me about, I really believe you're a unique fellow. Indeed, there has never been a person like you before, there is no one like you in the world now, and there never will be. See how much respect life has for you. You are a work of art. Impossible to replicate, incomparable, absolutely unique."

"Wow, Pranchú, what beautiful words! Can I add them to my reflections for my disciples this weekend? Actually, I'd like your authorization to use them in a book. Something like "You're unique, be proud of that!".

"Sure, feel free to share whatever you'd like. Honestly, you've published so many books that I have no idea when you have time to write in the middle of all that tantrism."

"Thanks, my dear Pranchú! You know, sharing is one of the highest spiritual qualities. The miracle is that the more joy you share, the more you have."

"Got it. Just be aware of how you share your wisdom, because sight is different for every eye."

"Oh, you don't have to explain that to me, old Pranchú, I know it very well. Now I must go because I have to prepare my six o'clock sermon. It was really nice to meet you here, in the middle of nowhere."

"Go with god, brother!" Pranchú replied.

Very well, Pranchú continued on his way and Osho on his. Months later, Pranchú received a letter from Osho in which he described the difficulties he was going through and the radicalism that had surged among some of his followers. He now recognized the importance of Pranchú's words from the day they'd met in the middle of nowhere. Osho also mentioned that one of his followers, *Ma Anand Sheela*, started spewing a bunch of nonsense in his name, but that she did not represent him in any way or form. He said the situation was nearly out of control.

Months later, Pranchú found out how insane Osho's life had become. Attacks, betrayals, imprisonments - any many other nouns, all plural. It was a plot worthy of a film of a "wild, wild country!" And it got worse. Osho was denied entry in more than twenty countries for they all saw him as a real-life pariah. In Western culture, this is akin to an outcast, someone excluded from social life. In Indian culture, however, it had a different, more intense meaning[75]. The only solution was to reverse his path and go back to old India.

Some years later, Pranchú sent Osho a letter to try to ease the anguish suffered by this passive subject. In the letter's last paragraph, as the story goes, Pranchú stated that which one day would be on a moral scroll:

"One who is not known must not be praised or offended. Therefore, rejoice! The persecutions you have suffered are similar to those suffered by other ancient prophets, which only strengthens your words. And these - the words - are involved in everything. They spark warmth in the spirit, delirium in the heart, and fire in the soul. Take a good look at yourself! The evil found in your words is not actually in them, but in the malicious ways in which they've been used. Thus, one should not fear those who listen and speak, but those who listen and are silent. This is the flux of nature and, in moments when reason is gone, here is a lesson you must never forget:

'Accept that on some days you are the pigeon and on other days you are the statue!'"

Legend has it that Osho read that letter, fell asleep, and never woke up again!

Thus said Pranchú!

---

[75] *A pariah, in Indian culture, is a term used to describe a person who does not belong to any caste, and is therefore considered impure and worthless in traditional Hindu culture. [Among the pariahs, mostly descendants of indigenous Indian tribes who refused to yield to Aryan rule, were bastards (whose parents were foreigners or from different castes), children of prostitutes, and those who had committed serious infractions against social or religious precepts]*

"WHILE THE BODY STILL
TAKES IN MORE BEER THAN
MEDICINE, THE BRAIN
WILL NEVER GIVE IN TO
INFIRMITIES!"

20

ADVICE FROM BUKOWSKI, THE OLD BASTARD

Addiction to drunkenness in youth accumulates reserves for the aches and pains of old age. This premise was taken very seriously by one of Pranchú's distant cousins who, as a result of destiny, lived in the American city of Los Angeles. The fellow, named Charles Bukowski, was born in Nazi Germany but had been living in the U.S., where he was raised, since the broken year of 1930.

Charles, or Buk as he was called, was such a unique fellow that he gave himself the nickname "Old Bastard" because he considered himself to be a drunk, lazy, and unpredictable womanizer. His stories were often about bottles of bourbon, beer, gin, wine, or some other liquor of bad quality. Also in bad quality was his health - he had problems in his liver, kidneys, lungs, and even hemorrhoids. Somehow he always found himself either a step away from the grave or from the slip of a banana peel.

Pranchú saw a lot of himself in Bukowski because of their shared interest in rascality, drunkenness, and, most of all, their extremely autobiographical character when writing manuscripts. Both were also victims of a natural social exclusion based on their physical traits, which made them forerunners in what one day would be called *bullying*, since they were targets of incessant jokes. If they were alive today, for instance, and were to ask in school what *bullying* meant, the teacher's reply would certainly be this:

"Class, look at the level of question these imbeciles asked me!"

Life's punches, however, help transform the most scatalogical experiences into important fuel for philosophical reflections. Even their shared ugliness was reason for cognition. Upon seeing Bukowski, Pranchú said: *"if it's not for beauty, may it be for philosophy!"* Everything was a reason for reflection amidst commotion, even more so if there was bourbon or cold beer! They were able to concentrate in the middle of any chaos and would later write about the experiences they had lived through.

Once, Pranchú decided to spend a few days at old Buk's house. They took the opportunity to go on binge of something they both highly enjoyed - drinking. To welcome Pranchú to his home, Buk invited some friends over and decided to have a typical L.A. barbecue, with a lot of hamburgers and barbecue sauce. Oh, how he missed sun dried meat! The talk around the grill leaned towards the disturbance in the LA streets and also about drinking beer with a hint of chive, but somehow always ended up on the subject of American literature. It was quite an eccentric conversation, Pranchú thought, but nothing short of what he had imagined.

A guy named Dutch, an old friend of Buk's who was at the barbecue, described the American poetry scene in a very curious way for that time:

"Almost all the greats (in poetry) have died recently. Frost, Cummings, Jeffers, W.C. Williams, T.S. Elliot, and others. The day before yesterday, it was Sandburg's turn, in such a short time. It's as if they all decided to go together!"

The conversation leaned towards this ultimate opinion: that we all are in the need of idols! Although this might have been discussed in the past, it can be repeated in the present. Despite their best efforts, Pranchú, Buk, and the other inebriate philosophers could not recognize any living idols. The drunkards even denounced current literature. That was the breaking point for Buk. The Old Bastard interrupted their ecstatic arguments and stated:

"Literature is like a woman: when it's not good, it's not worth your time."

Such a Chauvinist conclusion was enough to change the conversation and one day become one of old Buk's short stories[76].

Also on occasion of Pranchú's visit, old Buk would take him on trips to unhealthy places, such as the racetracks and libertine houses which, according to Buk, were places for the elderly. Upon arrival, Buk would immediately order his favorite drink: *Cold Turkey*. It was a drink made with bourbon (Wild Turkey) and Ice, simultaneously refreshing and burning. When he started to drink and smoke, Buk would often become a walking, philosophical machine gun. He did not care at all what others might think of him. He would say, paraphrasing Sartre, that "hell was other people". Life went from 0 to 60 in a matter of seconds.

After some heavy drinking which brought out the Old Bastard in him, Buk would

---

[76] Bukowski, Charles. *Cerveja, poetas e mais papo. In Fabulário Geral do Delírio Cotidiano: ereções, ejaculações e exibicionismo. Parte II*. Porto Alegre: L&PM, 2014, p. 170.

recite unusual poetry to the ladies working in those houses of debauchery. Poetry was a way to contemplate the mockery, but someday it would prove useful in his official writings, as if his ludicrousness could become literature. Buk would say to a lady:

"Oh, my dear old libertine
You're free and of dissolute rituals
Regardless, you'd still be a sybarite
Because you work for the mutual!"

The girl, even with a lack of understanding, would reply:

"Wow, Mr. Buk, I didn't get a single word of what you said, sir, but I thought it was beautiful. I'm going to give you a discount!"

After the allnighters and the customary hangovers, Buk always felt the need to write down the thoughts that had emerged the night before. Since his memory was being ruined by all the whiskey, he carried a small notebook which he affectionately nicknamed *the cretin*. It's also worth mentioning that old Buk drank heavily to deal with the aches and pains of old age, as he would often proclaim (initial assertive), and then right after would complain in his usual cantankerous tone:

"I don't know about other people, but me, when I reach down to put on my shoes every morning, I think - 'God Almighty, what else now? Life fucks me over, we don't get on well. We have to take one bite at a time, not eat everything at once. It's like swallowing buckets of shit[77]."

Was Old Buk complaining about his hangover or old age? In the end, it didn't matter. The fact was that Bukowski transformed his crazy life into masterful literature and was recognized for it during his lifetime. Pranchú was able to take part in this success from the sidelines, and it allowed him to have good reflections and learn wonders.

Discovering a cousin named Charles Bukowski who was a writer, made Pranchú realize he could also go back to writing since this gift might be in their blood. While at Buk's house, Pranchú took the chance to ask the Old Bastard if he would ever advise anyone to become a writer. Buk sharply replied:
"Writers are born writers. No advice would ever change that."

---

[77] Bukowski, Charles. *O Capitão saiu para o almoço e os marinheiros tomaram conta do navio*. Porto Alegre: L&PM, 2014, p. 14.

No sooner had he spoken than the Old Bastard realized how extremely disencouraging and pessimistic his thoughts were on what it meant to be a writer, especially considering his unruly personal life and the fact that he was speaking to Pranchú, the most skewed and shrewd philosopher in the region of Paraíba. Buk tried to assuage his sharp remark with a less intransigent argument:

"Listen, my friend! There is nothing that can stop a man from writing unless that man stops himself. Rejection and ridicule will only strengthen him. And the longer he is held back the stronger he will become, like a mass of rising water against a dam. There is no losing in writing, it will make your toes laugh as you sleep, it will make you stride like a tiger, it will fire the eye and put you face to face with Death. You will die a fighter, you will be honored in hell. The luck of the word. Go with it, send it. Be the Clown in the Darkness. It's funny[78]."

Each one of those words echoed in Pranchú's mind. In that instant, he remembered the conversation Buk and his pals had had on the day of the barbecue. Pranchú now saw in Bukowski the lost idolatry they had mentioned and came to realize how most people ignore their own capabilities. Old Buk wasn't a good example of anything at all, on the contrary, he was frequently seen as repugnant and lazy, but that didn't deprive him of his natural capability to self-impose when faced with life's difficulties. It was as if he could transform muddy, urban ennui and melancholy into inspiring rhapsodies.

To be a writer, according to Pranchú and within Bukowski's perspective, one can't just be a mere lover or enthusiast of literature. One must desire truth. That desire can be applied to all areas of life. If someone dreams of becoming a judge, they will be, if only they desire it. Being inventive is the chance! The biggest problem is that people don't actually know what they want, and so they never even try to do what they aim for. There is no such thing as desire in half. If you're willing to try, go on, as Bukowski would say:

If you're going to try,
go all the way.
Otherwise, don't even start!
This could mean losing girlfriends,

---

[78] Bukowski, Charles. *O Capitão saiu para o almoço e os marinheiros tomaram conta do navio.* Porto Alegre: L&PM, 2014, p. 23.

wives, relatives, work….maybe even your mind.
It could mean not eating for days,
It could mean freezing on a park bench,
It could mean jail,
It could mean mockery, isolation…
Isolation is the gift.
All the others are a test of your endurance,
of how much you really want to do it.
And, you'll do it, despite rejection and the worst odds.
And it will be better than anything else you can imagine.
If you're going to try,
go all the way.
There is no other feeling like that.
You will be alone with the gods,
and the nights will flame with fire.
You will ride life straight to perfect laughter.
It's the only good fight there is."

The act of creating, whether in the sciences or the arts, is the result of abnegation and surrender, and it will yield unimaginable fruit. Pranchú believed that the will to write would take him on unforgettable flights and immerse him in uncontrollable fires, especially if ignited by a good bottle of ethanol. There was no way to know the beginning or the end of this endeavor, but what truly mattered was the flight or the ink of a new paragraph. Each new line was a beginning that had nothing to do with the previous lines.

Bow to the wood and the stone, as each has its own enchantment, Bukowski would say to Pranchú. Draw from simpleness the beauty of things, in the same way that we are drawn from that simplicity. Thus, in plain objectivity, Pranchú welcomed the advice from a drunk Bukowski on how to get started in the enigmatic art of writing. Countering his shattered friend, Pranchú replied with one of his encyclical phrases, in the hopes that Buk would also not abandon his ideas:

"While the body still takes in more beer than medicine, the brain will never give in to infirmities!"

Thus said Pranchú!

The body of the text in this book was composed with fonts from the family Minion Pro, designed by Adobe. For titles, the Norse font, designed by artist Joël Carrouché, available at dafont.com